THE DAY AFTER JUDGMENT

JAMES BLISH was born in 1921 in East Orange, New Jersey. He studied microbiology at Rutgers University, graduating in 1942. He was drafted into Army service during World War II and discharged in 1944. After his discharge, Blish enrolled in a master's degree program at Columbia University but did not finish, opting to turn to fiction full-time instead. His first story appeared in *Super Science Stories* in 1940, and throughout the 1940s he would have a number of science fiction stories published in pulp magazines. The work for which he is perhaps best known, *Cities in Flight*, was published in four volumes between 1950 and 1962 and collected in a one-volume omnibus in 1970. His other major works include the *After Such Knowledge* series, which comprises *A Case of Conscience* (1958), winner of the Hugo Award, *Doctor Mirabilis* (1964), *Black Easter* (1968), and *The Day After Judgment* (1971), the latter two volumes available from Valancourt. Blish also wrote commercially successful novelizations and original novels based on the popular television series *Star Trek*.

He married literary agent Virginia Kidd in 1947, and after their divorce he married artist J. A. Lawrence, with whom he moved to England in 1968. Blish died of lung cancer in 1975.

Also available by James Blish

Black Easter

JAMES BLISH

The Day After Judgment

After such knowledge, what forgiveness?
T.S. Eliot

VALANCOURT BOOKS

Dedication: To Robert A. W. Lowndes
Text figures by Judith Ann Lawrence

The Day After Judgment by James Blish
Originally published by Doubleday in 1971
First Valancourt Books edition 2024

Copyright © 1971 by James Blish
A condensed version of this novel was published serially in *Galaxy Magazine*.
That version copyright © 1970, renewed 1998 by Judith L. Blish

All rights reserved. In accordance with the U.S. Copyright Act of 1976, the copying, scanning, uploading, and/or electronic sharing of any part of this book without the permission of the publisher constitutes unlawful piracy and theft of the author's intellectual property. If you would like to use material from the book (other than for review purposes), prior written permission must be obtained by contacting the publisher.

Published by Valancourt Books, Richmond, Virginia
http://www.valancourtbooks.com

The Valancourt Books name and logo are federally registered trademarks of Valancourt Books, LLC. All rights reserved

ISBN 978-1-960241-28-3 (case laminate hardcover)
978-1-960241-29-0 (trade paperback)
Also available as an electronic book.

Set in Adobe Jenson

STATIONS

The Wrath-Bearing Tree	11
So Above	21
Come to Middle Hell	55
The Harrowing of Heaven	95

PROLOGUE

The events leading up to the disaster were as follows:

Baines, president of Consolidated Warfare Service, the munitions subsidiary of an international chemical and dye cartel, applied to Theron Ware, a black magician of the highest repute, for a demonstration of his abilities. Accompanied by his executive assistant, Jack Ginsberg, a thoroughgoing skeptic, he visited Ware's rented palazzo in the Italian resort town of Positano, where Ware provided a minor exhibition of alchemy, changing two tears successively into blood, gold and lead under controlled circumstances.

This did not satisfy Baines, who had something much bigger in mind. Ware warned him that all magic, regardless of degree, is based upon the invocation of angels or demons—mostly the latter—and that it is expensive, dangerous and difficult. Baines already knew this from an earlier visit to Monte Albano, a sanctuary of white magicians. Strictly as a further test, Baines commissioned Ware to procure by magic the death of the current Governor of California. Ware agreed. Ginsberg, a man of slightly odd tastes, was intrigued by Ware's obvious confidence and in a private interview attempted to ask a favor of the magician, but did not succeed in specifying what it was. Ware offered him the use of a succubus, but was refused.

At Monte Albano, the white magicians had divined something of the nature of Baines's forthcoming major commission and had reason to believe that it might entail a major disaster for the whole world. Under the terms of the Grand Covenant under which all magic operates, they were entitled to impose upon Ware a white magician as an observer, provided that the white magician did not interfere in any way with Ware's operations. They chose Father Domenico, a suitably skilled and blameless man, who did not relish the assignment.

In the meantime, Baines, who had returned to Rome, received news of the death of the Governor of California, as specified. He decided to return to Positano, taking with him this time not only Jack Ginsberg, but also a scientist of his firm, Dr. Adolph Hess, also as an observer.

Thanks to various delays en route, Baines, Ginsberg, Hess and Father Domenico all arrived for the next invocation of Hell at the same time—during the Christmas season. Baines's second commission was a further test, this time the death of an eminent theoretical physicist with no known enemies. Ware agreed, and also consented to allow Baines's party to watch the process of invoking the demon involved; he barred Father Domenico, however. The monk subsequently divined that this in any case was not the major disaster he had been sent to observe. Prior to the experiment, Ware showed Hess, in whom he saw a potential ally, his laboratory and apparatus and explained to him some of the theory of magic. Hess was unwillingly impressed. Before the group, Ware then conjured up a demon named MARCHOSIAS, one of many with whom he had pacts, to tempt and destroy the next victim. It was a fearful process and left nobody in any doubt that Ware was exactly what he said he was: a human master of unthinkable infernal forces. Then all had to wait for the sending to take effect. During this period, Jack Ginsberg succeeded in expressing to Ware what it was that he wanted: to learn the Great Art. Ware, who by then had realized that Baines's next assignment was going to be so huge that he would have to have assistants, said he would consider this only if Jack would first sample the banquet he thought he wanted. At Ginsberg's assent, Ware did send him the previously proffered succubus, with the desired result: Jack was both revolted and captured—that is, he became addicted.

The victim of MARCHOSIAS duly died, and Baines revealed at last what had been in the back of his mind all the time:

"I would like to let all the major demons out of Hell for one night, turn them loose in the world with no orders and no restrictions, and see just what it is they would do if they were left on their own hooks like that." Baines's motive for wishing this was purely artistic; he was an aesthete of destruction, and his business had been increasingly failing to satisfy this side of his character.

Ware consented, but this time asked Father Domenico to be present at the ceremony, in case it should get out of control. Father Domenico had to agree, but pointed out that it would be safer if he could call together a whole convocation of white magicians at Monte Albano, to stand by in case of disaster. Ware, on reflection, decided that this was a wise precaution and assented.

Because of the time needed for preparations and for Father Domenico's trip, the experiment was scheduled for Easter. The white magicians, assembled from all over the world, in the meantime attempted to summon the aid of the Stewards of Heaven, but these archangelic demiurges Themselves turned out to be in some vast and incomprehensible confusion, so that it did not even prove possible to summon all seven of Them.

In a complex ceremony which lasted all night, Ware loosed upon the world forty-eight of the princes and presidents of Hell. The resulting destruction was more than extensive and imaginative enough to satisfy Baines, but well before dawn it became apparent that the experiment had indeed gotten out of hand, for World War III had broken out. Under the Covenant, Father Domenico was now empowered to demand that Ware recall the demons at once. To do this, Ware had to summon the prime minister of Hell, one LUCIFUGE ROFOCALE, as before; but this time was answered instead by one of the three chief princes of Hell, PUT SATANACHIA, sometimes called Baphomet, or the Sabbath Goat.

Hess, in a fatal mixture of terror and incredulity, broke out of his part of the magic circle, and the demon instantly destroyed him. It then revealed that Ware's last conjuration could not be undone, for it had unleashed Armageddon, and the forces of evil had been everywhere victorious. Father Domenico attempted to exorcise the creature, but at the attempt his crucifix shattered in his hands. The demon merely laughed, and after promising to return for them all in the morning, vanished, leaving behind three words:

"God is dead."

The Wrath-Bearing Tree

Woe, woe, woe to the inhabiters of the earth by reason of the other voices of the trumpet of the three angels, which are yet to sound!

REVELATION 8:13

The Fall of God put Theron Ware in a peculiarly unenviable position, though he was hardly alone. After all, he had caused it—insofar as an event so gigantic could be said to have had any cause but the First. And as a black magician he knew better than to expect any gratitude from the victor.

Nor, on the other hand, would it do him the slightest good to maintain that he had loosed the forty-eight suffragan demons upon the world only at the behest of a client. Hell was an incombustible Alexandrine library of such evasions—and besides, even had he had a perfect plea of innocence, there was no longer any such thing as justice, anywhere. The Judger was dead.

"When the hell *is* he coming back?" Baines, the client, demanded suddenly, irritably. "This waiting is worse than getting it over with."

Father Domenico turned from the refectory window, which was now unglazed, from the shock wave of the H-bombing of Rome. He had been looking down the cliff face, over the half-melted *pensioni*, shops and tenements of what had once been Positano, at the drained sea bed. When that tsunami did arrive, it was going to be a record one; it might even reach all the way up here.

"You don't know what you're saying, Mister Baines," the white magician said. "From now on, nothing can be over with. We are on the brink of eternity."

"You know what I mean," Baines growled.

"Of course, but if I were you, I'd be grateful for the respite . . . It *is* odd that he hasn't come back yet. Dare we hope that something has after all interfered with him? Something—or some One?"

"He said God is dead."

"Yes, but he is the Father of Lies. What do you think, Doctor Ware?"

Ware did not reply. The personage they were talking about was of course not the Father of Lies, the ultimate Satan, but the subsidiary prince who had answered Ware's last summons—PUT SATANACHIA, sometimes called Baphomet, the Sabbath Goat. As for the question, Ware simply did not know the answer; it was now sullen full morning of the day after Armageddon, and the Goat had promised to come for the four of them promptly at dawn, in ironical obedience to the letter of Ware's loosing and sending; yet he was not here.

Baines looked around the spent conjuring room. "I wonder what he did with Hess?"

"Swallowed him," Ware said, "as you saw. And it served the fool right for stepping outside of his circle."

"But did he really eat him?" Baines said. "Or was that, uh, just symbolical? Is Hess actually in Hell now?"

Ware refused to be drawn into the discussion, which he recognized at once as nothing but Baines's last little vestige of skepticism floundering about for an exit from its doom; but Father Domenico said,

"The thing that called itself Screwtape let slip to Lewis that demons do eat souls. But one can hardly suppose that that is the end. I expect we will shortly know a lot more about the matter than we wish."

Abstractedly, he brushed from his robe a little more of the dust from his shattered crucifix. Ware watched him with ironic wonder. He really was staging a remarkable recovery; his God was dead, his Christ as exploded as a myth, his soul assuredly as damned as that of Ware or Baines—and yet he could still manage to interest himself in semi-Scholastic prattle. Well, Ware had always thought that white magic, these days as always, attracted only a low order of intellect, let alone insight.

But where *was* the Goat?

"I wonder where Mister Ginsberg went?" Father Domenico said, as if in parody of Ware's unspoken question. Again, Ware only shrugged. He had for the moment quite forgotten Baines's male secretary; it was true that Ginsberg had shown some promise as an apprentice, but after all, he had wanted to learn the Ars Magica essentially as a means of supplying himself with mistresses, and even under normal circumstances his recent experience with Ware's assistant, Gretchen—who was in fact a succubus—had probably driven the desire out permanently. In any event, of what use would an apprentice be now?

Baines looked as startled as Ware felt at the question. "Jack?" he said. "I sent him to our rooms to pack."

"To pack?" Ware said. "You had some notion that you might get away?"

"I thought it highly unlikely," Baines said evenly, "but if the opportunity arose, I didn't mean to be caught unprepared."

"Where do you think you might go where the Goat couldn't find you?"

No reply was necessary. Ware felt through his sandals a slow shuddering of the tiled floor. As it grew more pronounced, it was joined by a faint but deep thunder in the air.

Father Domenico shuffled hastily back to the window, Baines close behind him. Unwillingly, Ware followed.

On the horizon, a wall of foaming, cascading water was coming toward them with preternatural slowness, across the deserted floor of the Tyrrhenian Sea. The water had all been drained away as one consequence of the Corinth earthquake of yesterday, which itself might or might not have been demonically created; Ware was not sure that it made much difference one way or the other. In any event, the tectonic imbalance was now, inexorably, in the process of righting itself.

The Goat remained unaccountably delayed ... but the tsunami was on its way at last.

What had been Jack Ginsberg's room in the palazzo now looked a great deal more like the cabinet of Dr. Caligari. Every stone, every window frame, every angle, every wall was out of true, so that there was no place to stand where he did not feel as though he had been imprisoned in a tesseract—except that even the planes of the prison were crazed with jagged cracks without any geometry whatsoever.

The window panes were out, and the ceiling dripped; the floor was invisible under fallen plaster, broken glass and anonymous dirt; and in the *gabinetto* the toilet was pumping continuously as though trying to flush away the world. The satin-sheeted bed was sandy to the touch, and when he took his clothes out of the wardrobe, his beautiful clothes so carefully selected from *Playboy*, dust fumed out of them like spores from a puffball.

There was no place to lay clothes out but on the bed, though it was only marginally less filthy than any other flat surface available. He wiped down the outside of his suitcase with a handkerchief, which he then dropped out the window down the cliff, and began to stow things away, shaking them out with angry coughs as best he could.

The routine helped, a little. It was not easy to think about any other part of this incredible impasse. It was even difficult to know whom to blame. After all, he had known about Baines's creative impulse toward destruction for a long time and had served it; nor had he ever thought it insane. It was a common impulse: to one engineer you add one stick of dynamite, and in the name of progress he will cut a mountain in half and cover half a country with concrete, for no better real reason than that he enjoys it. Baines was only the same kind of monomaniac, writ large because he had made so much money at it; and unlike the others, he had always been honest enough to admit that he did it because he loved the noise and the ruin. More generally, top management everywhere, or at least back in the States, was filled with people who loved their business, and cared for nothing else but crossword puzzles or painting by the numbers.

As for Ware, what had he done? He had prosecuted an art to his own destruction, which was traditionally the only sure way a life can be made into a work of art. Unlike that idiot Hess, he had known how to protect himself from the minor unpleasant consequences of his fanaticism, though he had turned out to be just as blindly suicidal in the end. Ware was still alive, and Hess was dead—unless his soul still lived in Hell—but the difference now was only one of degree, not of kind. Ware had not invited Baines's commission; he had only hoped to use it to enlarge his own knowledge; as Hess had been using Baines; as Baines had used Hess and Ware to satisfy his business and aesthetic needs; as Ware and Baines had used Jack's administrative talents and his delight in straight, raw sex; as Jack had tried to use them all in return.

They had all been things, not people, to each other, which after all is the only sensible and fruitful attitude in a thing-dominated world. (Except, of course, for Father Domenico, whose desire to prevent anybody from accomplishing anything, chiefly by wringing his hands, had to be written off as the typical, incomprehensible attitude of the mystic—a howling anachronism in the modern world, and predictably ineffectual.) And in point of fact none of them—not even Father Domenico—could fairly be said to have failed. Instead, they had all been betrayed. Their plans and operations had all depended implicitly upon the existence of God—even Jack, who had entered Positano as an atheist, had been reluctantly forced to grant that—and in the final pinch, He had turned out to have been not around any more after all. If this shambles was anyone's fault, it was His.

He slammed down the cover of his suitcase. The noise was followed, behind him, by a fainter sound, about halfway between the clearing of a throat and the sneeze of a cat. For a moment he stood stock-still, knowing very well what that sound meant. But it was useless to ignore it, and finally he turned around.

The girl was standing on the threshold, as before, and as before, she was somewhat different. It was one of the immemorial snares of her type; at each apparition she seemed like someone else, and yet always, at the same time, reminded him of someone—he could never think who—he had once known; she was always at once mistress, harem and stranger. Ware ironically called her Gretchen, or Greta, or Rita, and she could be compelled by the word *Cazotte*, but in fact she had no name, nor even any real sex. She was a demon, alternately playing succubus to Jack and incubus to some witch on the other side of the world. In theory only, the idea of such a relationship would have revolted Jack, who was fastidious, in his fashion. In actual practice, it did indeed revolt him ... insufficiently.

"You do not make me as welcome as before," she said.

Jack did not reply. This time the apparition was blond again, taller than he was, very slender, her hair long and falling straight down her back. She wore a black silk sari with gold edging, which left one breast bare, and gold sandals, but no jewelry. Amidst all this rubble, she looked fresh as though she had just stepped out of a tub: beautiful, magical, terrifying and irresistible.

"I thought you could come only at night," he said at last.

"Oh, those old rules are gone forever," she said, and as if to prove it, stepped across the threshold without even one invitation, let alone three. "And you are leaving. We must celebrate the mystery once more before you go, and you must make me a last present of your seed. It is not very potent; my other client is thus far disappointed. Come, touch me, go into me. I know it is your need."

"In this mess? You must have lost your mind."

"Nay, impossible; intellect is all I am, no matter how I appear to you. Yet am I capable of monstrous favors, as you know well, and will to know again."

She took the suitcase, which was still unfastened, off the bed and set it flat on the floor. Though it was almost too heavy for Jack when fully loaded, handling it did not appear to cost her the slightest effort. Then, lifting one arm and with it the bare and spiky breast, she unwound the sari in a single, continuous sweeping motion, and lay down naked across the gritty bed, light glinting from dewdrops caught about her inflamed mound, a vision of pure lubricity.

Jack ran a finger around the inside of his collar, though it was open. It was impossible not to want her, and at the same time he wanted desperately to escape—and besides, Baines was waiting, and Jack had better sense than to pursue his hobby on company time.

"I should have thought you'd be off raising hell with your colleagues," he said, his voice hoarse.

The girl frowned suddenly, reminding him of that fearful

moment after their first night when she had thought that he had been mocking her. Her fingernails, like independent creatures, clawed slowly at her flat abdomen.

"Dost think to copulate with fallen seraphim?" she said. "I am not of any of the Orders which make war; I do only what would be hateful even to the damned." Then, equally suddenly, the frown dissolved in a little shower of laughter. "And ah, besides, I raise not Hell, but the Devil, for already I have Hell in me—dost know that story of Boccaccio?"

Jack knew it; there was no story of that kind he did not know; and his Devil was most certainly raised. While he still hesitated, there was a distant growling sound, almost inaudible but somehow also infinitely heavy. The girl turned her head toward the window, also listening; then she looked back at him, spread her thighs and held out her arms.

"I think," she said, "that you had better hurry."

With a groan of despair, he fell to his knees and buried his face in her muff. Her smooth legs closed about his ears; but no matter how hard he pulled at her cool, pliant rump, the sound of the returning sea rose louder and louder around them both.

So Above

Haeresis est maxima opera maleficarum non credere.
 —Heinrich Institor and Jakob Sprenger:
 Malleus Maleficarum

I

The enemy, whoever he was, had obviously been long prepared to make a major attempt to reduce the Strategic Air Command's master missile-launching control site under Denver. In the first twenty minutes of the war, he had dumped a whole stick of multiple hydrogen warheads on it. The city, of course, had been utterly vaporized, and a vast expanse of the plateau on which it had stood was now nothing but gullied, vitrified and radioactive granite; but the site had been well hardened and was more than a mile beneath the original surface. Everybody in it had been knocked down and temporarily deafened, there were bruises and scrapes and one concussion, some lights had gone out and a lot of dust had been raised despite the air conditioning; in short, the damage would have been reported as "minimal" had there been anybody to report it to.

Who the enemy was occasioned some debate. General D. Willis McKnight, a Yellow Peril fan since his boyhood reading of *The American Weekly* in Chicago, favored the Chinese. Of his two chief scientists, one, the Prague-born Dr. Džejms Šatvje, the godfather of the selenium bomb, had been seeing Russians under his bed for almost as long.

"Nu, why argue?" said Johann Buelg. As a RAND Corporation alumnus, he found nothing unthinkable, but he did not like to waste time speculating about facts. "We can always ask the computer—we must have enough input already for that. Not that it matters much, since we've already plastered the Russians *and* the Chinese pretty thoroughly."

"We already know the Chinese started it," General McKnight said, wiping dust off his spectacles with his handkerchief. He was a small, narrow-chested Air Force Academy graduate from the class just after the cheating had been stopped, already nearly bald at forty-eight; naked, his face looked remarkably like that of a prawn. "They dropped a thirty-megatonner on Formosa, disguised as a test."

"It depends on what you mean by 'start,'" Buelg said. "That was already on Rung twenty-one, Level Four—local nuclear war. But still only Chinese against Chinese."

"But we were committed to them, right?" Šatvje said. "President Agnew told the UN, 'I am a Formosan.'"

"It doesn't matter worth a damn," Buelg said, with some irritation. It was his opinion, which he did not keep particularly private, that Šatvje, whatever his eminence as a physicist, in all other matters had a *goyische kopf*. He had encountered better heads on egg creams in his father's candy store. "The thing's escalated almost exponentially in the past eighteen hours or so. The question is, how far has it gone? If we're lucky, it's only up to Level Six, central war—maybe no farther than Rung thirty-four, constrained disarming attack."

"Do you call atomizing Denver 'restrained?'" the General demanded.

"Maybe. They could have done for Denver with one warhead, but instead they saturated it. That means they were shooting for us, not for the city proper. Our counterstrike couldn't be preventive, so it was one rung lower, which I hope to God they noticed."

"They took Washington out," Šatvje said, clasping his fat hands piously. He had been lean once, but becoming first a consultant on the Cabinet level, next a spokesman for massive retaliation, and finally a publicity saint had appended a beer belly to his brain-puffed forehead, so that he now looked like a caricature of a nineteenth-century German philologist. Buelg himself was stocky and tended to run to lard, but a terrible susceptibility to kidney stones had kept him on a reasonable diet.

"The Washington strike almost surely wasn't directed against civilians," Buelg said. "Naturally the leadership of the enemy is a prime military target. But, General, all this happened so quickly that I doubt that anybody in government had a chance to reach prepared shelters. You may now be effectively the president of whatever is left of the United States, which means that you could make new policies."

"True," McKnight said. "True, true."

"In which case we've got to know the facts the minute our lines to outside are restored. Among other things, if the escalation's gone all the way to spasm, in which case the planet will be uninhabitable. There'll be nobody and nothing left alive but people in hardened sites, like us, and the only policy we'll need for that will be a count of the canned beans."

"I think that needlessly pessimistic," Šatvje said, at last heaving himself up out of the chair into which he had struggled after getting up off the floor. It was not a very comfortable chair, but the computer room—where they had all been when the strike had come—had not been designed for comfort. He put his thumbs under the lapels of his insignia-less adviser's uniform and frowned down upon them. "The Earth is a large planet, of its class; if we cannot reoccupy it, our descendants will be able to do so."

"After five thousand years?"

"You are assuming that carbon bombs were used. Dirty bombs of that kind are obsolescent. That is why I so strongly advocated the sulfur-decay chain; the selenium isotopes are chemically all strongly poisonous, but they have very short half-lives. A selenium bomb is essentially a *humane* bomb."

Šatvje was physically unable to pace, but he was beginning to stump back and forth. He was again playing back one of his popular magazine articles. Buelg began to twiddle his thumbs, as ostentatiously as possible.

"It has sometimes occurred to me," Šatvje said, "that our discovery of how to release the nuclear energies was providential. Consider: Natural selection stopped for Man when he achieved control over his environment, and furthermore began to save the lives of all his weaklings, and preserve their bad genes. Once natural selection has been halted, then the only remaining pressure upon the race to evolve is mutation. Artificial radioactivity, and indeed even fallout itself, may be God's way of resuming the process of evolution for

Man... perhaps toward some ultimate organism we cannot foresee, perhaps even toward some unitary mind which we will share with God, as Teilhard de Chardin envisioned—"

At this point, the General noticed the twiddling of Buelg's thumbs.

"Facts are what we need," he said. "I agree with you there, Buelg. But a good many of our lines to outside *were* cut, and there may have been some damage to the computer circuitry, too." He jerked his head toward the technicians who were scurrying around and up and down the face of RANDOMAC. "I've got them working on it. Naturally."

"I see that, but we'll need some sort of rational schedule of questions. Is the escalation still going on, presuming we haven't reached the insensate stage already? If it's over, or at least suspended somehow, is the enemy sane enough not to start it again? And then, what's the extent of the exterior damage? For that, we'll need a visual readout—I assume there are still some satellites up, but we'll want a closer look, if any local television survived.

"And if you're now the president, General, are you prepared to negotiate, if you've got any opposite numbers in the Soviet Union or the People's Republic?"

"There ought to be whole sets of such courses of action already programmed into the computer," McKnight said, "according to what the actual situation is. Is the machine going to be useless to us for anything but gaming, now that we really need it? Or have you been misleading me again?"

"Of course I haven't been misleading you. I wouldn't play games with my own life as stakes. And there are indeed such alternative courses; I wrote most of them myself, though I didn't do the actual programming. But no program can encompass what a specific leader might decide to do. War gaming actual past battles—for example, rerunning Waterloo without allowing for Napoleon's piles, or the heroism of the British squares—has produced 'predicted' outcomes completely at variance with history. Computers are rational; people aren't. Look at Agnew. That's why I asked you my question—which, by the way, you haven't yet answered."

McKnight pulled himself up and put his glasses back on.

"I," he said, "am prepared to negotiate. With anybody. Even Chinks."

II

Rome was no more, nor was Milan. Neither were London, Paris, Berlin, Bonn, Tel Aviv, Cairo, Riyadh, Stockholm and a score of lesser cities. But these were of no immediate concern. As the satellites showed, their deaths had expectably laid out long, cigar-shaped, overlapping paths of fallout to the east—the direction in which, thanks to the rotation of the Earth, the weather inevitably moved—and though these unfortunately lay across once friendly terrain, they ended in enemy country. Similarly, the heavy toll in the U.S.S.R. had sown its seed across Siberia and China; that in China across Japan, Korea and Taiwan; and the death of Tokyo was poisoning only a swath of the Pacific (although, later, some worry would have to be devoted to the fish). Honolulu somehow had been spared, so that no burden of direct heavy nuclei fallout would reach the West Coast of the United States.

This was fortunate, for Los Angeles, San Francisco, Portland, Seattle and Spokane had all been hit, as had Denver, St. Louis, Minneapolis, Chicago, New Orleans, Cleveland, Detroit and Dallas. Under the circumstances, it really hardly mattered that Pittsburgh, Philadelphia, New York, Syracuse, Boston, Toronto, Baltimore and Washington had all also gotten it, for even without the bombs, the Eastern third of the continental United States would have been uninhabitable in its entirety for at least fifteen years to come. At the moment, in any event, it consisted of a single vast forest fire through which, from the satellites, the slag pits of the bombed cities were invisible except as high spots in the radiation contours. The Northwest was in much the same shape, although the West Coast in general had taken far fewer missiles. Indeed, the sky all over the world was black with smoke, for the forests of Europe and northern Asia were burning, too. Out of the pall, more death fell, gently, invisibly, inexorably.

All this, of course, came from the computer analysis. Though there were television cameras in the satellites, even on a clear day you could hardly have told from visual sightings, from that height—nor from photographs, for that matter—even whether or not there was intelligent life on Earth. The view over Africa, South America, Australia and the American Southwest was better, but of no strategic or logistic interest, and never had been.

Of the television cameras on the Earth's surface, most of the surviving ones were in areas where nothing seemed to have happened at all, although in towns the streets were deserted, and the very few people glimpsed briefly on the screen looked haunted. The views from near the bombed areas were fragmentary, traveling, scarred by rasters, aflicker with electronic snow—a procession of unconnected images, like scenes from an early surrealist film, where one could not tell whether the director was trying to portray a story or only a state of mind.

Here stood a single telephone pole, completely charred; here was a whole row of them, snapped off at ground level but still linked in death by their wires. Here was a desert of collapsed masonry, in the midst of which stood a reinforced-concrete smokestack, undamaged except that its surface was etched by heat and by the sand blasting of debris carried by a high wind. Here buildings all leaned sharply in a single direction, as if struck like the chimney by some hurricane of terrific proportions; here was what had been a group of manufacturing buildings, denuded of roofing and siding, nothing but twisted frames. Here a row of wrecked automobiles, neatly parked, burned in unison; here a gas holder, ruptured and collapsed, had burned out hours ago.

Here was a side of a reinforced concrete building, windowless, cracked and buckled slightly inward where a shock wave had struck it. Once it had been painted gray or some dark color, but all the paint had blistered and scaled and blown away in a second, except where a man had been standing nearby; there the paint remained, a shadow with no one to cast it.

That vaporized man had been one of the lucky. Here stood another who had been in a cooler circle: evidently he had looked up at a fireball, for his eyes were only holes; he stood in a half crouch, holding his arms out from his sides like a penguin, and instead of skin, his naked body was covered with a charred fell which was cracked in places, oozing blood and pus. Here a filthy, tattered mob clambered along a road almost completely covered with rubble, howling with horror—though there was no sound with this scene—led by a hairless woman pushing a flaming baby carriage. Here a man who seemed to have had his back flayed by flying glass worked patiently with a bent snow shovel at the edge of an immense mound of broken brick; by the shape of its margins, it might once have been a large house.

There was more.

Šatvje uttered a long, complex, growling sentence of hatred. It was entirely in Czech, but its content was nevertheless not beyond all conjecture. Buelg shrugged again and turned away from the TV screen.

"Pretty fearful," he said. "But on the whole, not nearly as much destruction as we might have expected. It's certainly gone no *higher* than Rung thirty-four. On the other hand, it doesn't seem to fit any of the escalation frames at all well. Maybe it makes some sort of military or strategic sense, but if it does, I'm at a loss to know what it is. General?"

"Senseless," McKnight said. "Outright senseless. Nobody's been hurt in any *decisive* way. And yet the action seems to be over."

"That was my impression," Buelg agreed. "There seems to be some missing factor. We're going to have to ask the computer to scan for an anomaly. Luckily it's likely to be a big one—but since I can't tell the machine what *kind* of anomaly to look for, it's going to cost us some time."

"How much time?" McKnight said, running a finger around the inside of his collar. "If the Chinks start up on us again—"

"It may be as much as an hour, after I formulate the question and Chief Hay programs it, which will take, oh, say two hours at a minimum. But I don't think we need to worry about the Chinese; according to our data, that opening Taiwan bomb was the biggest one they used, so it was probably the biggest one they had. As for anyone else, well, you just finished saying yourself that somehow everything's now stopped short. We badly need to find out why."

"All right. Get on it, then."

The two hours for programming, however, stretched to four; and then the computer ran for ninety minutes without producing anything at all. Chief Hay had thoughtfully forbidden the machine to reply DATA INSUFFICIENT, since new data were coming in at an increasing rate as communications with the outside improved; as a result, the computer was recycling the problem once every three or four seconds.

McKnight used the time to issue orders that repairs to the keep be made, stores assessed, order restored, and then settled down to a telecommunications search—again via the computer, but requiring only about 2 percent of its capacity—for any superiors who might have survived him. Buelg suspected that he really wanted to find some; he had the capacity to be a general officer, but would find it most uncomfortable to be a president, even over so abruptly simplified a population and economy—and foreign policy, for that matter—as the TV screen had shown now existed outside. Ordering junior officers to order noncommissioned officers to order rankers to replace broken fluorescent bulbs was the type of thing he didn't mind doing on his own, but for ordering them to arm missiles and aim them, or put a state under martial law, he much preferred to be acting upon higher authority.

As for Buelg's own preference, he rather hoped that McKnight wouldn't be able to find any such person. The United States under a McKnight regime wouldn't be run very imaginatively or even flexibly, but on the other hand it would be unlikely to be a tyranny. Besides, McKnight was very dependent upon his civilian experts, and hence would be easy to manage. Of course, that meant that something would have to be done about Šatvje—

Then the computer rang its bell and began to print out its analysis. Buelg read it with intense concentration, and after the first fold, utter incredulity. When it was all out of the printer, he tore it off, tossed it onto the desk and beckoned to Chief Hay.

"Run the question again."

Hay turned to the input keyboard. It took him ten minutes to retype the program; the question had been in the normal order of things too specialized to tape. Two and a half seconds after he had finished, the machine chimed and the long thin slabs of metal began to rise against the paper. The printing-out process never failed to remind Buelg of a player piano running in reverse, converting notes into punches instead of the other way around, except, of course, that what one got here was not punches but lines of type. But he saw almost at once that the analysis itself was going to be the same as before, word for word.

At the same time he became aware that Šatvje was standing just behind him.

"About time," the Czech said. "Let's have a look."

"There's nothing to see yet."

"What do you mean, there's nothing to see? It's printing, isn't it? And you've already got another copy out on the bench. The General should have been notified immediately."

He picked up the long, wide accordion fold of paper with its sprocket-punched edges and began to read it. There was nothing Buelg could do to prevent him.

"The machine's printing nonsense, that's what I mean, and I didn't propose to distract the General with a lot of garbage. The bombing must have jarred something loose."

Hay turned from the keyboard. "I ran a test program through promptly after the attack, Doctor Buelg. The computer was functioning perfectly then."

"Well, clearly it isn't now. Run your test program again, find out where the trouble lies, and let us know how long it will take to repair it. If we can't trust the computer, we're out of business for sure."

Hay got to work. Šatvje put the readout down.

"What's nonsense about this?" he said.

"It's utterly impossible, that's all. There hasn't been time. With any sort of engineering training, you'd know that yourself. And it makes no military or political sense, either."

"I think we should let the General be the judge of that."

Picking up the bulky strip again, Šatvje carried it off toward the General's office, a certain subtle triumph in his gait, like the school trusty bearing the evidence of petty theft to the head master. Buelg followed, inwardly raging, and not only at the waste motion. Šatvje would of course tell McKnight that Buelg had been holding back on reporting the analysis; all Buelg could do now, until the machine was repaired, was to be sure to be there to explain why, and the posture was much too purely defensive for his liking. It was a damn shame that he had ever taught Šatvje to read a printout, but once they had been thrown together on this job, he had had no choice in the matter. McKnight had been as suspicious as a Sealyham of both of them, anyhow, at the beginning. Šatvje, after all, had come from a country which had long been Communist, and had had to explain that his ancestry was French, his name only a Serbo-Croat transliteration back from the Cyrillic of "Chatvieux"; while Security had unfortunately confused Buelg with Johann Gottfried Julg, a forgotten nineteenth-century translator of *Ardshi Bordschi Khan*, the *Siddhi Kur*, the *Skaskas* and other Russian folk tales, so that Buelg, even more demeaningly, had had to admit that his name was actually a Yiddish version of a German word for a leather bucket. Under McKnight's eye, the two still possibly suspect civilians had to cooperate or be downgraded into some unremunerative university post. Buelg supposed that Šatvje had enjoyed it as little as he had, but he didn't care an iota about what Šatvje did or didn't enjoy. Damn the man.

As for the document itself, it was no masterpiece of analysis. The machine had simply at last recognized an anomaly in a late-coming piece of new data. It was the interpretation that made Buelg suspect that the gadget had malfunctioned; unlike Šatvje, he had had enough experience of computers at RAND to know that if they were not allowed enough warm-up time, or had been improperly cleared of a previous program, they could produce remarkably paranoid fantasies.

Translated from the Fortran, the document said that the United States had not only been hit by missiles, but also deeply invaded. This conclusion had been drawn from a satellite sighting of something in Death Valley, not there yesterday, which was not natural, and whose size, shape and energy output suggested an enormous fortress.

"Which is just plain idiotic," Buelg added, after the political backing and filling in McKnight's office had been gone through, to nobody's final advantage. "On any count you care to name. The air drops required to get the materials in there, or the sea landings plus overland movements, couldn't have gone undetected. Then, strategically it's insane: the building of targets like fortresses should have become obsolete with the invention of the cannon, and the airplane made them absurd. Locating such a thing in Death Valley means that it dominates nothing but utterly worthless territory, at the price of insuperable supply problems—right from the start it's in a state of siege, by Nature alone. And as for running it up overnight—I ask you, General, could *we* have done that, even in peacetime and in the most favorable imaginable location? I say we couldn't, and that if we couldn't, no human agency could."

McKnight picked up his phone and spoke briefly. Since it was a Hush-a-Phone, what he said was inaudible, but Buelg's guess about the call was promptly confirmed.

"Chief Hay says the machine is in perfect order and has produced a third analysis just like this one," he reported. "The problem now clearly is one of reconnaissance. [He pronounced the word correctly, which, amidst his flat California American, sounded almost affected.] Is there such a thing in Death Valley, or isn't there? For the satellite to be able to spot it at all, it must be gigantic. From twenty-three thousand miles up, even a city the size of San Antonio is invisible unless you know exactly what you're looking for in advance."

Here, Buelg was aware, McKnight was speaking as an expert. Until he had been put in charge of SAC in Denver, almost all his career had been spent in various aspects of Air Information; even as a teenager, he had been a Civil Air Patrol cadet involved in search-and-rescue operations, which, between the mudslides and the brushfires, had been particularly extensive in the Los Angeles area in those days.

"I don't doubt that the satellite has spotted *something*," Buelg said. "But what it probably 'sees' is a hard-radiation locus—maybe thermally hot, too—rather than any optical object, let alone a construct. My guess is that it's nothing more than the impact site of a multiple warhead component that lost guidance, or was mis-aimed to begin with."

"Highly likely," McKnight admitted. "But why guess? The obvious first step is to send a low-level attack bomber over the site and get close-in photographs and spectra. A primitive installation such as you suggested earlier would be typically Chinese, and if so they won't have low-level radar. If on the other hand the plane gets shot down, that will tell us something about the enemy, too."

Buelg sighed inwardly. Trying to nudge McKnight out of his single channel was a frustrating operation. But maybe, in this instance, it wasn't really necessary; after all, the suggestion itself was sensible.

"All right," he said. "One plane seems like a small investment. We've got damn all else left to lose now, anyhow."

III

No attack was made on the plane, but there was nevertheless one casualty. Neither the photographer nor the flight engineer, both busy with their instruments, had actually seen much of the target, and the Captain, for the same reason, had seen little more.

"Hell of a lot of turbulence," he said at the debriefing, which took place a thousand miles away, while the men under Denver watched intently. "And the target itself is one huge updraft, like New York used to be, only much worse."

But the navigator, once his job had been done, had had nothing to do but look out, and he was in a state of shock. He was a swarthy young enlisted man from Chicago who looked as though he might have been recruited straight from a Mafiosa family, but he could say nothing now but a sentence which refused to get beyond its first syllable: "Dis—Dis—" Once he had recovered from his shock they would be able to question him. But for the time being he was of no help.

The photographs, however, were very clear, except for the infrared sensitive plates, which showed nothing intelligible to the eye at all. The installation was perfectly circular and surrounded by a moat which, impossibly for Death Valley, appeared to be filled with black but genuine water, from which a fog bank was constantly trying to rise, only to be dissipated in the bone-dry air. The construction itself was a broad wall, almost a circular city, a good fifteen miles in diameter. It was broken irregularly by towers and other structures, some of them looking remarkably like mosques. This shell glowed fiercely, like red-hot iron, and a spectrograph showed that this was exactly what it was.

Inside, the ground was terraced, like a lunar crater. At ground level was a flat plain, dotted with tiny rectangular markings in no discernible pattern; these, too, the spectrograph said, were red-hot iron. What seemed to be another moat, blood-red and as broad as a river, encircled the next terrace at the foot of the cliff where it began, and this, even more impossibly, was bordered by a dense circular forest. The forest was as broad as the river, but thinned eventually to a ring of what appeared to be the original sand, equally broad.

In a lunar crater, the foothills of the central peak would have begun about here, but in the pictures, instead, the terrain plunged into a colossal black pit. The river cut through the forest and the desert at one point and roared over the side in a vast waterfall, compounding the darkness with mist which the camera had been unable to penetrate.

"What was that you were saying about building a fortress overnight, Buelg?" the General said. "'No human agency could?'"

"No human agency was involved," Šatvje said in a hoarse whisper. He turned to the aide who had brought the pictures, an absurdly young lieutenant colonel with a blond crew cut, white face and shaking hands. "Are there any close-ups?"

"Yes, Doctor. There was an automatic camera under the plane that took a film of the approach run. Here is one of the best shots."

The picture showed what appeared to be a towering gate in the best medieval style. Hundreds of shadowy figures crowded the barbican, of which three, just above the gateway itself, had been looking up at the plane and were shockingly clear. They looked like gigantic naked women, with ropy hair all awry, and the wide-staring eyes of insane rage.

"I thought so," Šatvje said.

"You recognize them?" Buelg asked incredulously.

"No, but I know their names: Alecto, Megaera and Tisiphone," Šatvje said. "And it's a good thing that there's at least one person among us with a European education. I presume that our *distrait* friend the navigator is a Catholic, which does just as well in this context. In any event, he was quite right: this is Dis, the fortress surrounding Nether Hell. I think we must now assume that all the rest of the Earth is contiguous with Upper Hell, not only in metaphor but in fact."

"It's a good thing," Buelg said acidly, "that there's at least one person among us with a good grip on his sanity. The last thing we need now is a relapse into superstition."

"If you blow up that photograph, I think you'll find that the hair on those women actually consists of live snakes. Isn't that so, Colonel?"

"Well ... Doctor, it ... it certainly looks like it."

"Of course. Those are the Furies who guard the gates of Dis. They are the keepers of the Gorgon Medusa, which, thank God, isn't in the picture. The moat is the River Styx; the first terrace inside contains the burning tombs of the Heresiarchs, and on the next you have the River Phlegethon, the Wood of the Suicides, and the Abominable Sand. A rain of fire is supposed to fall continually on the sand, but I suppose that's invisible in Death Valley sunlight or maybe even superfluous. We can't see what's down below, but presumably that too will be exactly as Dante described it. The crowd along the barbican is made up of demons—not so, Colonel?"

"Sir ... we can't tell what they are. We were wondering if they were, well, Martians or something. Every one is a different shape."

Buelg felt his back hairs stirring. "I refuse to believe this nonsense," he said. "Šatvje is interpreting it from his damned obsolete 'education.' Even Martians would make more sense."

"What are the facts about this Dante?" McKnight said.

"An Italian poet, of about the thirteenth century—"

"Early fourteenth," Šatvje said. "And not just any poet. He had a vision of Hell and Heaven which became the greatest poem ever written—the *Divine Comedy*. What we see in those pictures exactly corresponds to the description in Cantos Eight through Eleven of it."

"Buelg, see if you can locate a copy of the book and have it read to the computer. First we need to know if the correspondence is all that exact. If it is, we'll need an analysis of what it means."

"The computer probably already has the book," Buelg said. "The whole Library of Congress, plus all our recreational library, is on microfilm inside it, we didn't have room for books per se down here. All we need to do is tell Chief Hay to make it part of the problem. But I still think it's damn nonsense."

"What we want," McKnight said, "is the computer's opinion. Yours has already been shown to be somewhat less reliable."

"And while you're at it," Šatvje said, perhaps a shade less smugly than Buelg might have expected, "have Chief Hay make a part of the problem everything in the library on demonology. We're going to need it."

Throwing up his hands, Buelg left the office. In the country of the mad ...

Nobody retains his sanity.

Only a few moments were needed for the computer to produce its report:

THE ANCIENT TEXTS AND FICTIONS NOW ADMITTED TO THE PROBLEM DISAGREE WITH EACH OTHER. HOWEVER, THE NEW FACTUAL DATA MAKE EXACT MATCHES WITH A NUMBER OF THEM, AND APPROXIMATE MATCHES WITH THE MAJORITY OF THEM. THE ASSUMPTION THAT THE CONSTRUCT IN DEATH VALLEY IS RUSSIAN, CHINESE OR OTHERWISE OF HUMAN ORIGIN IS OF THE LOWEST ORDER OF PROBABILITY AND MAY BE DISCOUNTED. THE INTERPLANETARY HYPOTHESIS IS OF SLIGHTLY HIGHER PROBABILITY, AN INVASION FROM VENUS BEING COMPATIBLE WITH A FEW OF THE FACTUAL DATA, SUCH AS THE IMMENSE HEAT AND ABERRANT LIFE FORMS OF THE DEATH VALLEY INSTALLATION, BUT IS INCOMPATIBLE WITH MOST ARCHITECTURAL AND OTHER HISTORICAL DETAILS IN THE DATA, AS WELL AS WITH THE LEVEL OF TECHNOLOGY INDICATED. THE PROBABILITY THAT THE DEATH VALLEY INSTALLATION IS THE CITY OF DIS AND THAT ITS INTERNAL AREA IS NETHER HELL IS 0.1 WITHIN A 5% LEVEL OF CONFIDENCE, AND THEREFORE MUST BE ADMITTED. AS A FIRST DERIVATIVE, THE PROBABILITY THAT THE WAR JUST CONCLUDED WAS ARMAGEDDON IS 0.01 WITHIN THE SAME CONFIDENCE LEVEL. AS A SECOND DERIVATIVE, THE PROBABILITY THAT THE SURFACE OF THE EARTH IS NOW CONFLUENT WITH UPPER HELL IS 0.001 WITHIN THE SAME CONFIDENCE LEVEL.

"Well, that clarifies the situation considerably," McKnight said. "It's just as well we asked."

"But—my God!—it simply can't be true," Buelg said desperately. "All right, maybe the computer is functioning properly, but it has no intelligence, and above all, no judgment. What it's putting out now is just a natural consequence of letting all that medieval superstition into the problem."

McKnight turned his shrimp's eyes toward Buelg. "You've seen the pictures," he said. "They didn't come out of the computer, did they? Nor out of the old books, either. I think we'd better stop kicking against the pricks and start figuring out what we're going to do. We've still got the United States to think of. Doctor Šatvje, have you any suggestions?"

That was a bad sign. McKnight never used honorifics except to indicate, by inversion, which of the two of them had incurred his displeasure—not that Buelg had been in any doubt about that, already.

"I'm still in a good deal of doubt," Šatvje said modestly. "To begin with, if this has been Armageddon, we all ought to have been called to judgment by now; and there was certainly nothing in the prophecies that allowed for an encampment of victorious demons on the surface of the Earth. If the computer is completely right, then either God is dead as Nietzsche said, or, as the jokes go, He is alive but doesn't want to get involved. In either case, I think we would be well advised not to draw attention to ourselves. We can do nothing against supernatural powers; and if He *is* still alive, the battle may not be over. We are, I hope, safely hidden here, and we would be ill advised to be caught in the middle."

"Now there you're dead wrong," Buelg said with energy. "Let's suppose for a minute that this fantasy represents the true state of affairs—in other words, that demons have turned out to be real, and are out there in Death Valley—"

"I'm none too sure what would be meant by 'real' in this context," Šatvje said. "They are apparent, true enough; but they certainly don't belong to the same order of reality as—"

"That's a question we can't afford to debate," Buelg said. He knew very well that the issue Šatvje was raising was a valid one—he was himself a fairly thoroughgoing Logical Positivist. But it would only confuse McKnight, and there were brownie points to be made in keeping things clear-cut, whether they *were* clear-cut or not. "Look. If demons are real, then they occupy space/time in the real universe. That means that they exist inside some energy system in that universe and are maintained by it. All right, they can walk on red-hot iron and live comfortably in Death Valley; that's not inherently more supernatural than the existence of bacteria in the boiling waters of volcanic springs. It's an adaptation. Very well, then we can find out what that energy system is. We can analyze how it works. And once we know that, we can attack it."

"Now that's more like it," McKnight said.

"Pardon me, but I think we should proceed with the most extreme caution," Šatvje said. "Unless one has been raised in this tradition, one is not likely to think of all the implications. I myself am quite out of practice at it."

"Damn your education," Buelg said. But it was all coming back to him: The boundaryless ghetto along Nostrand Avenue; the fur-hatted, fur-faced, maxi-skirted Hassidim walking in pairs under the scaling elm saplings of Grand Central Parkway; the terror of riding the subway among the juvenile gangs under the eternal skullcap; the endless hairsplitting over the Talmudic and Midrashic creation myths for hour upon stuffy hour in *Schule*; the women slaving over their duplicate sets of dishes, in the peculiar smell of a kosher household, so close to being a stench compared to all other American smells, supporting their drone scholars; his mother's pride that Hansli too was plainly destined by God's will to become a holy man; and when he had discovered instead the glories and rigors of the physical universe, that light and airy escape from fur hats and the smell of gefuelte fish and the loving worn women, the terror of the wrath of the jealous God. But all that was many years ago; it could not come back. He would not have it back.

"What are you talking about?" McKnight said. "Are we going to do something, and if so, what? Get to the point."

"My point," Šatvje said, "is that if all this—demonology—is, well, valid, or I suppose one should say true, then the whole Christian mythos is true, though it is not coming out in precisely the way it was prophesied. That being the case, then there are such things as immortal souls, or perhaps I should say, we may well have immortal souls, and we ought to take them into consideration before we do anything rash."

Buelg saw the light, and with a great sense of relief; the Christian mythos had nothing to do with him, not personally, that is. He had no objection to it as an exercise in theory, a form of non-zero-sum game.

"If that's the case, I don't think there's any question of our being caught in the middle," he said. "We're required by the rules to come down on one side or the other."

"That's true, by God," McKnight said. "And after all, we're on the right side. We didn't start this war—the Chinks did."

"Right, right," Buelg said. "We're entitled to self-defense. And for my part, no matter what happens in the next world—about which we have no data—as long as I'm still in this one, I'm not prepared to regard *anything* as final. This may be a metaphysical war after all, but we still seem to live in some sort of secular universe. The universe of discourse has been enlarged, but it hasn't been canceled. I say, let's find out more about it."

"Yes," McKnight said, "but how? That's what I keep asking, and I don't get anything back from either of you but philosophical discussion. What do you propose that we *do?*"

"Have we got any missiles left?"

"We've still got maybe a dozen five- to ten-megatonners left—and, of course, Old Mombi."

"Buelg, you madman, are you proposing for one instant—"

"Shut up for a minute and let me think." Old Mombi was Denver's doomsday machine, a complex carrier containing five one hundred-megaton warheads, one of which was aimed to make even the Moon uninhabitable; it was a post-spasm weapon that the present situation certainly did not call for—best to hold it in reserve. "I think what we ought to do is to lob one of the small jobs onto the Death Valley encampment. I don't really think it'll do much harm, maybe not any, but it might produce some information. We can fly a drone plane through the cloud as it goes up, and take off radiological, chemical, any other kinds of readings that the computer can come up with. These demons have obtruded themselves into the real world, and the very fact that we can see them and photograph them shows that they share some of its characteristics now. Let's see how they behave under something a good deal hotter than red-hot iron. Suppose they do nothing more than sweat a little? We can analyze even that!"

"And suppose they trace the missile back to here?" Šatvje said, but by his expression, Buelg knew that Šatvje knew that it was a last-ditch argument.

"Then we're sunk, I suppose. But look at the architecture of that encampment; does that suggest to you that they've been in contact with real warfare since back in the fourteenth century? No doubt they have all kinds of supernatural powers, but they've got a lot to learn about the natural ones! Maybe a decent adversary is what they've been lacking all along—and if Armageddon has ended in a standoff, a little action on the side of our Maker wouldn't be amiss. If He's still with us, and actively interested, any *in*action on our parts would probably be viewed very gravely indeed if He wins after all. And if He's not with us any longer, then we'll have to help ourselves, as the proverb says."

"That's the stuff to give the troops," McKnight said. "It is so ordered."

Buelg nodded and left the office to search out Chief Hay. On the whole, he felt, he had made a nice recovery.

IV

Positano had been washed away, but the remains of Ware's palazzo still stood above the scoured cliffside, like some post-Roman ruin. The ceiling had fallen in, the fluted pink tiles smashing Ware's glassware and burying the dim chalk diagrams of last night's conjuration on the refectory floor in a litter of straw and potsherds, mounds of which collapsed now and then to send streamers of choking dust up to meet the gently radioactive April rain.

Ware sat on the heaped remains of his altar within the tumbled walls, under the uncertain sky. His feelings were so complex that he could not have begun to explain them, even to himself; after many years' schooling in the rigorous non-emotions of Ceremonial

Magic, it was a novelty to him to have any feelings at all but those of the thirst for knowledge; now he would have to relearn those sensations, for his lovely book of acquisitions, upon which he had spent his soul and so much else, was buried under tons of tsunamic mud.

In a way, he thought tentatively, he felt free. After the shock of the seaquake had passed, and all but an occasional tile had stopped falling, he had struggled out of the rubble to the door, and thence to the head of the stairway which led down to his bedroom, only to see nothing but mud three stone steps down, mud wrinkling and settling as the sea water gradually seeped out from under it. Somewhere down under there, his book of new knowledge was beginning the aeon-long route to becoming an unreadable fossil. Well then; so much for his life. Almost it seemed to him then that he might begin again, that he was nameless, a *tabula rasa*, all false starts wiped out, all dead knowledge ready to be rejected or revivified. It was given to few men to live through something so cleansing as a total disaster.

But then he realized that this, too, was only an illusion. His past was there, ineluctably, in his commitments. He was still waiting for the return of the Sabbath Goat. He closed the door to the stairwell and the fossilized ripples of the mud, and blowing reflectively into his white mustache, went back into the refectory.

Father Domenico had earlier tired—it could not exactly be said that he had lost patience—of both the waiting and the fruitless debates over when or whether they would be come for, and had decided to attempt traveling south to see what and who remained of Monte Albano, the college of white magicians which had been his home grounds. Baines was still there, trying to raise some news on the little transistor radio to which only yesterday he had listened so gluttonously to the accounts of the Black Easter which Ware had raised up at his commission, and whose consequences now eddied away from them around the whole tortured globe. Now, however, it was producing nothing but bands of static, and an occasional very distant voice in an unknown tongue.

With him now was Jack Ginsberg, dressed to the nines as usual, and in consequence looking by far the most bedraggled of the three. At Ware's entrance, Baines tossed the radio to his secretary and crossed toward the magician, slipping and cursing the rubble.

"Find out anything?"

"Nothing at all. As you can see for yourself, the sea is subsiding. It is obvious that Positano has been spared any further destruction—for the moment. As for why, we know no more than we did before."

"You can still work magic, can't you?"

"I don't appear to have been deprived of my memory," Ware said. "I've no doubt I can still *do* magic, if I can get at my equipment under this mess, but whether I can work it is another matter. The conditions of reference have changed drastically, and I have no idea how far or in what areas."

"Well, you could at least call up a demon and see if he could give us any information. There doesn't appear to be anyone else to ask."

"I see that I'll have to put the matter more bluntly. I am totally opposed to performing any more magic at this time, Doctor Baines. I see that you have again failed to think the situation through. The terms under which I was able to call upon demons no longer apply—I am no longer able to do anything for them, they must now own a substantial part of the world. If I were to call at this juncture, probably no one would answer, and it might be better if nobody did, since I would have no way of controlling him. They are composed almost entirely of hatred for every unFallen creature, and every creature with the potentiality to be redeemed, but there is no one they hate more than a useless tool."

"Well, it seems to me that we may neither of us be totally useless even now," Baines declared. "You say the demons now own a substantial part of the world, but it's also perfectly evident that they don't own it all yet. Otherwise the Goat would have come back when he said he would. And we'd be in Hell."

"Hell has a great many circles. We may well be on the margins of the first right now—in the Vestibule of the Futile."

"We'd be in a good deal deeper if the demons were in total control, or if judgment had already been passed on us," Baines said.

"You are entirely right about that, to be sure," Ware said, somewhat surprised. "But after all, from their point of view there is no hurry. In the past, we might have saved ourselves by a last-minute act of contrition. Now, however, there is no longer any God to appeal to. They can wait and take us at their leisure."

"There I'm inclined to agree with Father Domenico. We don't know that for sure; we were told so only by the Goat. I admit that the other evidence all points in the same direction, but all the same, he could have been lying."

Ware thought about it. The argument from circumstances did not of course impress him; no doubt the circumstances were horrible beyond the capacity of any human soul to react to them, but they were certainly not beyond the range of human imagination; they were more or less the standard consequences of World War III, a war which Baines himself had been actively engaged in engineering some time before he had discovered his interest in black magic. Theologically they were also standard: a new but essentially unchanged version of the Problem of Evil, the centuries-old question of why a good and merciful God should allow so much pain and terror to be inflicted upon the innocent. The parameters had been filled in a somewhat different way, but the fundamental equation was the same as it had always been.

Nevertheless, the munitions maker was quite right—as Father Domenico had been earlier—to insist that they had no reliable information upon the most fundamental question of all. Ware said slowly:

"I'm reluctant to admit any hope at all at this juncture. On the other hand, it has been said that to despair of God is the ultimate sin. What precisely do you have in mind?"

"Nothing specific yet. But suppose for the sake of argument that the demons are still under some sort of restrictions—I don't see any point in trying to imagine what they might be—and that the battle consequently isn't really over yet. If that's the case, it's quite possible that they could still use some help. Considering how far they've managed to get already, there doesn't seem to be much doubt about their winning in the end—and it's been my observation that it's generally a good idea to be on the winning side."

"It is folly to think that the triumph of evil could ever be a winning side, in the sense of anyone's gaining anything by it. Without good to oppose it, evil is simply meaningless. That isn't at all what I thought you had in mind. It is, instead, the last step in despairing of God—it's worse than Manicheanism, it is Satanism pure and simple. I once controlled devils, but I never worshiped them, and I don't plan to begin now. Besides—"

Abruptly, the radio produced a tearing squeal and then began to mutter urgently in German. Ware could hear the voice well enough to register that the speaker had a heavy Swiss accent, but not well enough to make out the sense. He and Baines took a crunching step toward Ginsberg, who, listening intently, held up one hand toward them.

The speech was interrupted by another squeal, and then the radio resumed emitting nothing more than snaps, crackles, pops and waterfalls. Ginsberg said:

"That was Radio Zurich. There's been an H-bomb explosion in the States, in Death Valley. Either the war's started again, or some dud's gone off belatedly."

"Hmm," Baines said. "Well, better there than here ... although, now that I come to think of it, it isn't entirely unpromising. But Doctor Ware, I think you hadn't quite finished?"

"I was only going to add that 'being of some help' to demons in this context makes no practical sense, either. Their hand is turned against everyone on Earth, and there is certainly no way that we could help them to carry their war to Heaven, even presuming that any of Heaven still stands. Someone of Father Domenico's school might just possibly manage to enter the Aristotelian spheres— though I doubt it—but I certainly couldn't."

"That bomb explosion seems to show that *somebody* is still fighting back," Baines said. "Providing that Jack isn't right about its being a dud or a stray. My guess is that it's the Strategic Air Command, and that they've just found out who the real enemy is. They had the world's finest data processing center there under Denver, and in addition, McKnight had first-class civilian help, including Džejms Šatvje himself, and a RAND man that I tried to get the Mamaroneck Research Institute to outbid the government for."

"I still don't quite see where that leaves us."

"I know McKnight very well; he's steered a lot of Defense Department orders my way, and I was going to have LeFebre make him president of Consolidated Warfare Service when he retired— as he was quite well aware. He's good in his field, which is reconnaissance, but he also has something of a one-track mind. If he's bombing demons, it might be a very good idea for me to suggest to him that he stop it—and why."

"It might at that," Ware said reflectively. "How will you get there?"

"A technicality. Radio Zurich is still operating, which almost surely means that their airfield is operating too. Jack can fly a plane if necessary, but it probably won't be necessary; we had a very well-staffed office in Zurich, in fact it was officially our central headquarters, and I've got access to two Swiss bank accounts, the company's and my own. I'd damn well better put the money to some use before somebody with a little imagination realizes that the vaults might much better be occupied by himself, his family and twenty thousand cases of canned beans."

The project, Ware decided, had its merits. At least it would rid him, however temporarily, of Baines, whose society he was beginning to find a little tiresome, and of Jack Ginsberg, whom he distantly but positively loathed. It would of course also mean that he would be deprived of all human company if the Goat should after all come for him, but this did not bother him in the least; he had known for years that in that last confrontation, every man is always alone, and most especially, every magician.

Perhaps he had also always known, somewhere in the deepest recesses of his mind, that he would indeed eventually take that last step into Satanism, but if so, he had very successfully suppressed it. And he had not quite taken it yet; he had committed himself to nothing, he had only agreed that Baines should go away, and Ginsberg too, to counsel someone he did not know to an inaction which might be quite without significance....

And while they were gone, perhaps he would be able to think of something better. It was the tiniest of small hopes, and doubtless vain; but now he was beginning to be prepared to feed it. If he played his cards right, he might yet mingle with the regiment of angels who rebelled not, yet avowed to God no loyalty, of whom it is said that deep Hell refuses them, for, beside such, the sinner would be proud.

V

Monte Albano, Father Domenico found with astonishment and a further rekindling of his hope, had been spared completely. It reared its eleventh-century walls, rebuilt after the earthquake then by the abbot Giorgio who later became Pope John the Twentieth, as high above the valley as it always had, and as always, too, accessible only by muleback, and Father Domenico lost more time in locating a mule with an owner to take him up there than the whole trip from Positano had cost him. Eventually, however, the thing was done, and he was within the cool walls of the library with the white monks, his colleagues under the hot Frosinian sky.

Those assembled made up nearly the same company that had met during the winter to consider, fruitlessly, how Theron Ware and his lay client might be forestalled: Father Amparo, Father Umberto (the director), and the remaining brothers of the order, plus Father Uccello, Father Boucher, Father Vance, Father Anson, Father Selahny and Father Atheling. The visitors had apparently continued to stay in the monastery, if not in session, after the winter meeting, although in the interim Father Rosenblum had died; his place had been taken, though hardly filled, by Father Domenico's former apprentice, Joannes, who though hardly seventeen looked now as though he had grown up very suddenly. Well, that was all right; they surely needed all the help that they could get, and Father

Domenico knew without false modesty that Joannes had been well trained.

After Father Domenico had been admitted, announced and conducted through the solemn and blessed joys of greeting and welcome, it became apparent that the discussion—as was only to have been expected—had already been going on for many hours. Nor was he much surprised to find that it was simply another version of the discussion that had been going on in Positano: namely, how had Monte Albano been spared in the worldwide catastrophe, and what did it mean? But in this version of the discussion, Father Domenico could join with a much better heart.

And in fact he was also able to give it what amounted to an entirely new turn; for their Sensitive, the hermit-Father Uccello, had inevitably found his talents much coarsened and blunted by the proximity of so many other minds, and in consequence the white monks had only a general idea of what had gone on in Ware's palazzo since the last convocation—an impression supplemented by the world news, what of it there was, and by deduction, some of which was in fact wrong. Father Domenico recapitulated the story of the last conjuration briefly; but his fellows' appreciation of the gravity of the situation was already such that the recitation was accompanied by no more than the expectable number of horrified murmurs.

"All in all," he concluded, "forty-eight demons were let out of the Pit as a result of this ceremony, commanded to return at dawn. When it became apparent that the operation was completely out of hand, I invoked the Covenant and insisted that Ware recall them ahead of time, to which he agreed; but when he attempted to summon up LUCIFUGE ROFOCALE, to direct this abrogation, PUT SATANACHIA himself answered instead. When I attempted to exorcise this abominable creature, my crucifix burst in my hands, and it was after that that the monster told us that God was already dead and that the ultimate victory had instead gone to the forces of Hell. The Goat promised to return for us all—all, that is, except Baines's other assistant, Doctor Hess, whom Baphomet had already swallowed when Hess panicked and stepped out of his circle—at dawn, but he failed to do so, and I subsequently left and came to Monte Albano as soon as it was physically possible for me to do so."

"Do you recall the names and offices of all forty-eight?" said Father Atheling, his tenor voice more sinusy than ever with apprehension.

"I think I do—that is, I think I could; after all, I saw them all, and that's an experience which does not pass lightly from the memory. In any event, if I've blanked out on a few—which isn't unlikely either—they can doubtless be recovered under hypnosis. Why does that matter, may I ask, Father Atheling?"

"Simply because it is always useful to know the natures, as well as the numbers, of the forces arrayed against one."

"Not after the countryside is already overrun," said Father Anson. "If the battle and the war have been already lost, we must have the whole crew to contend with now—not just all seventy-two princes, but every single one of the fallen angels. The number is closer to seven and a half million than it is to forty-eight."

"Seven million, four hundred and fifty thousand, nine hundred and twenty-six," Father Atheling said, "to be exact."

"Though the wicked may hide, the claws of crabs are dangerous people in bridges," Father Selahny intoned abruptly. As was the case with all his utterances, the group would doubtless find out what this one meant only after sorting out its mixed mythologies and folklores, and long after it was too late to do anything about it. Nor did it do any good to ask him to explain; these things simply came to him, and he no more understood them than did his hearers. If God was indeed dead, Father Domenico wondered suddenly, Who could be dictating them now? But he put the thought aside as non-contributory.

"There is a vast concentration of new evil on the other side of the world," Father Uccello said in his courtly, hesitant old man's voice. "The feeling is one of intense oppression, quite different from that which was common in New York or Moscow, but one such as I would expect of a massing of demons upon a huge scale. Forgive me, brothers, but I can be no more specific."

"We know you are doing the best you can," said the director soothingly.

"I can feel it myself," said Father Monteith, who although not a Sensitive had had some experience with the herding of rebellious spirits. "But even supposing that we do not have to cope with so large an advance, as I certainly hope we do not, it seems to me that forty-eight is too large a sum for us if the Covenant has been voided. It leaves us without even an option."

Father Domenico saw that Joannes was trying to attract the director's attention, although too hesitantly to make any impression. Father Umberto was not yet used to thinking of Joannes as a person at all. Capturing the boy's eyes, Father Domenico nodded.

"I never did understand the Covenant," the ex-apprentice said, thus encouraged. "That is, I didn't understand why God would compromise Himself in such a manner. Even with Job, He didn't make a deal with Satan, but only allowed him to act unchecked for a certain period of time. And I've never found any mention of the Covenant in the grimoires. What are its terms, anyhow?"

Father Domenico thought the question well asked, if a trifle irrelevant, but an embarrassed and slightly pitying silence showed that his opinion was not shared. In the end it was broken by Father Monteith, whose monumental patience was a byword in the chapter.

"I'm certainly not well versed in canon law, let alone in spiritual compacts," he said, with more modesty than exactness. "But, in principle, the Covenant is no more than a special case of the option of free will. The assumption appears to be that even in dealing with devilry, on the one hand, no man shall be subjected to a temptation beyond his ability to resist, and on the other, no man shall slide into Heaven without having been tempted up to that point. In situations involving Transcendental or Ceremonial Magic, the Covenant is the line drawn in between. Where you would find its exact terms, I'm sure I don't know; I doubt that they have ever been written down. One thinks of the long struggle to understand the rainbow, the other Covenant; once the explanation was in, it did not explain, except to show that every man sees his own rainbow, and what seems to stand in the sky is an optical illusion, not a theomorphism. It is in the nature of the arrangement that the terms would vary in each individual case, and that if you are incapable of determining where it is drawn for you—the line of demarcation—then, woe betide you, and that is that."

Dear God, Father Domenico thought, all my life I have been an amateur of Roger Bacon and I never once saw that that was what he meant to show by focusing his *Perspectiva* on the rainbow. Shall I have any more time to learn? I hope we are never tempted to make Monteith the director, or we shall lose him to taking things out of the In box and putting them into the Out box, as we did Father Umberto—

"Furthermore, it may well be still in existence," said Father Boucher. "As Father Domenico has already pointed out to Theron Ware himself, we have heard of the alleged death of God only through the testimony of the most unreliable witness imaginable. And it leaves many inconsistencies to be explained. *When* exactly is God supposed to have died? If it was as long ago as in Nietzsche's time, why had His angels and ministers of light seemed to know nothing of it in the interim? It's unreasonable to suppose that they were simply keeping up a good front until the battle actually broke out; Heaven simply isn't that kind of an organization. One would expect an absolute and perpetual monarchy to break down upon the death of the monarch quite promptly, yet in point of fact we saw no signs of any such thing until shortly after Christmas of this year."

"But we did see such signs at that time," Father Vance said.

"True, but this only poses another logical dilemma: What happened to the Antichrist? Baphomet's explanation that he had been dispensed with as unnecessary to the victors, whose creature he would have been, doesn't hold water. The Antichrist was to have appeared *before* the battle, and if the defeat of God is all that recent, the prophecy should have been fulfilled; God still existed to compel it."

"Matthew 11:14," Father Selahny said, in an unprecedented

burst of intelligibility. The verse of which he was reminding them referred to John the Baptist, and it said: *And if ye will receive it, this is Elias, which was for to come.*

"Yes," Father Domenico said, "I suppose it's possible that the Antichrist might have come unrecognized. One always envisioned people flocking to his banner openly, but the temptation would have been more subtle and perhaps more dangerous had he crept past us, say in the guise of some popular philosopher, like that positive-thinking man in the States. Yet the proposal seems to allow even less room than did the Covenant for the exercise of free will."

There was a silence. At last, the director said: "The Essenes argued that one must think and experience all evil before one can even hope to perceive good."

"If this be true doctrine," Father Domenico said, "then it follows that God is indeed still alive, and that Theron Ware's experiment, and World War Three, did not constitute Armageddon after all. What we may be confronted with instead is an Earthly Purgatory, from which Grace, and perhaps even the Earthly Paradise, might be won. Dare we think so?"

"We dare not think otherwise," said Father Vance. "The question is, how? Little that is in the New Testament, the teachings of the Church or the Arcana seem very relevant to the present situation."

"No more is our traditional isolation," said Father Domenico. "Our only recourse now is to abandon it; to abandon our monastery and our mountain, and go down into the world that we renounced when Charlemagne was but a princeling, to try to win it back by works and witnessing. And if we may not do this with the sweet aid of Christ, then we must nevertheless do it in His name. Hope now is all we have."

"In sober truth," Father Boucher said quietly, "that is not so great a change. I think it is all we ever had."

Come to Middle Hell

Though thy beginning was small, yet thy latter end should greatly increase.... Prepare thyself to the search.

JOB 8:7, 8

VI

Left to his own devices and hence, at last, unobserved, Theron Ware thought that it might be well, after all, if he did essay a small magic. The possible difficulty lay in that all magic without exception depended upon the control of demons, as he had explained to Baines on his very first visit. But therein lay the attractiveness of the experiment, too, for what he wanted was information, and a part of that information was whether he still had any such control.

And it would also be interesting, and possible to find out at the same time, to know whether or not there were any demons left in Hell. If there were it would imply, though it would not guarantee, that only the forty-eight that he had set loose were now terrorizing the world. This ruled out using the Mirror of Solomon, for the spirit of that mirror was the Angel Anaël. Probably he would not answer anyhow, for Ware was not a white magician, and had carefully refrained from calling upon any angel ever since he had turned to the practice of the black Art; and besides, it would be a considerable nuisance locating three white pigeons amidst all this devastation.

Who, then? Among the demon princes he had decided not to call up for Baines's commission were several that he had ruled out because of their lesser potentialities for destruction, which would stand him in good stead were it to turn out that he had lost control; even in Hell there were degrees of malevolence, as of punishment. One of these was PHOENIX, a poet and teacher with whom Ware had had many dealings in the past, but he probably would not do now; he posed another wildlife problem—Ware's familiar Ahktoi had been the demon's creature, and the cat had of course vanished when the noise had begun, a disappearance that PHOENIX would take nonetheless ill for its having been 100 percent expectable. Though the grimoires occasionally characterize one or another demon as "mild" or "good by nature," these terms are strictly relative and have no human meaning; all demons are permanently enraged by the greatest Matter of all, and it does not pay to annoy them even slightly in small matters.

Also, Ware realized, it would have to be a small magic indeed, for most of his instruments were now buried, and those that were accessible were all contaminated beyond his power to purify them in any useful period of time. Clearly it was time to consult the book. He crossed to the lectern upon which it rested, pushed dust and potsherds off it with his sleeve, unlocked the clasp and began to turn the great stiff pages, not without a qualm. Here, signed with his own blood, was half his life; the other half was down below, in the mud.

He found the name he needed almost at once: VASSAGO, a mighty prince, who in his first estate before the rebellion had belonged to the choir of the Virtues. The *Lemegeton* of the Rabbi Solomon said of him, Ware recalled, that he "declares things past, present and future, and discovers what has been lost or hidden." Precisely to the purpose. Ware remembered too that his was the name most commonly invoked in ceremonial crystallomancy, which would be perfect in both scope and limitations for what Ware had in mind, involving no lengthy preparations of the operator, or even any precautionary diagrams, nor any apparatus except a crystal ball; and even for that he might substitute a pool of exorcised water, fifty liters of which still reposed in a happily unruptured stainless steel tank imbedded in the wall behind Ware's workbench.

Furthermore, he was the only demon in Ware's entire book of pacts who was represented therein by two seals or characters, so markedly different that without seeing them side by side one might never suspect that they belonged to the same entity. Topologically they were closely related, however, and Ware studied these relationships long and hard, knowing that he had once known what they meant but unable to recall it. These were the figures:

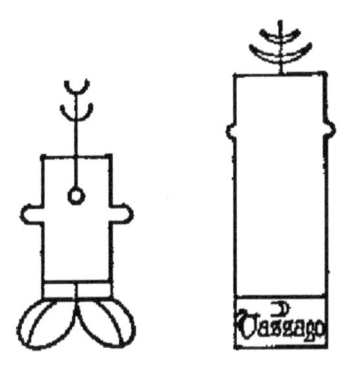

Ah, now he had it. The left-hand figure was Vassago's ordinary infernal sign, but the second was the seal under which, it was said, he could be called by white magicians. Ware had never used it, nor had needed to—the infernal seal had worked very well—and he had always doubted its efficacy, for by definition no commerce with a demon is white magic; however, it would be well to try it now. It might provide an additional factor of safety, if it worked at all.

Into what should he draw the water? Everything was filthy. Eventually he decided simply to make a puddle on the workbench; it had been decades since he had studied oneirology, which he had scorned as a recourse for mere hedge wizards, but to the best of his recollection it called for nothing more extraordinary than an earthenware vessel, and could even be practiced successfully in an ordinary, natural forest pool, providing that there was sufficient shade.

Well, then, to work.

Standing insecurely before the workbench, the little weight of his spare upper body resting upon his elbows and his hands beside his ears, Theron Ware stared steadfastly down into the little puddle of mud, his own bushy head—he had neglected his tonsure since the disaster—shading it from the even light of the overcast sky. He had already stared so long since the first invocation that he felt himself on the verge of self-hypnosis, but now, he thought, there was a faint stirring down there in those miniature carboniferous depths, like a bubble or a highlight created by some non-existent sun. Yes, a faint spark was there, and it was growing.

"*Eka, dva, tri, chatur, pancha, shas, sapta, ashta, navu, dasha, eka-dasha,*" Ware counted. "*Per vota nostra ipse nunc surtat nobis dicatus* Vassago!"

The spark continued to grow until it was nearly the size of a ten-lire piece, stabilized, and gradually began to develop features. Despite its apparent diameter, the thing did not look small; the effect rather was one of great distance, as though Ware were seeing a reflection of the Moon.

The features were quite beautiful and wholly horrible. Superficially the shining face resembled a human skull, but it was longer, thinner, more triangular, and it had no cheekbones. The eyes were huge, and slanted almost all the way up to where a human hairline would have been; the nose extremely long in the bridge; the mouth as pink and tiny as that of an infant. The color and texture of the face were old ivory, like netsuke. No body was visible, but Ware had not expected one; this was not, after all, a full manifestation, but only an apparition.

The rosebud mouth moved damply, and a pure soprano voice, like that of a choirboy, murmured gently and soundlessly deep in Ware's mind.

Who is it calls Vassago from studying of the damned? Beware!

"Thou knowest me, demon of the Pit," Ware thought, "for to a pact hast thou subscribed with me, and written into my book thine Infernal name. Thereby, and by thy seal which I do here exhibit, do I compel thee. My questions shalt thou answer, and give true knowledge."

Speak and be done.

"Art still in Hell with thy brothers, or are all abroad about the Earth?"

Some do go to and fro, but we abide here. Nevertheless, we be on Earth, albeit not abroad.

"In what wise?"

Though we may not yet leave Nether Hell, we be among ye: for the Pit hath been raised up, and the City of Dis now standeth upon the Earth.

Ware made no attempt to disguise his shock; after all, the creature could see into his mind. "How situate?" he demanded.

Where she stood from eternity; in the Valley of Death.

Ware suspected at once that the apparently allegorical form of this utterance concealed a literal meaning, but it would do no good to ask for exact topographical particulars; demons paid little attention to Earthly political geography unless they were fomenting strife about boundaries or enclaves, which was not one of Vassago's roles. Could the reference be literary? That would be in accordance with the demon's nature. Nothing prevents devils from quoting scripture to their own advantage, so why not Tennyson?

"Be this valley under the Ambassadorship of Rimmon?"

Nay.

"Then what officers inhabit the region wherein it lies? Divulge their names, great prince, to my express command!"

They are the inferiors of Astaroth, who are called Sargatanas and Nebiros.

"But which hath his asylum where Dis now stands?"

There ruleth Nebiros.

These were the demons of post-Columbian magic; they announced forth to the subjects all things which their lord hath commanded, according to the *Grimorium Verum*, in America, and the asylum of Nebiros was further specified to be in the West. Of course: Death Valley. And Nebiros, as it was said in the *Grand Grimoire*, was the field marshal of Infernus, and a great necromancer, "who goeth to and fro everywhere and inspects the hordes of perdition." The raising of the fortress of Dis in the domain of this great general most strongly suggested that the war was not over yet. Ware knew better, however, than to ask the demon whether God was in fact dead; for were He not, the mere sounding of the

Holy Name would so offend this minor prince as to terminate the apparition at once, if not render further ones impossible. Well, the question was probably unnecessary anyhow; he already had most of the information that he needed.

"Thou art discharged."

The shining face vanished with a flash of opalescence, exactly as though a soap bubble had broken, leaving Ware staring down at nothing but a puddle of mud, now already filming and cracking—except in the center where the face had been; that had evaporated completely. Straightening his aching back, he considered carefully the implications of what he had learned.

The military organization of the Descending Hierarchy was peculiar, and as usual the authorities differed somewhat on its details. This was hardly surprising, for any attempt to relate the offices of the evil spirits to Earthly analogues was bound to be only an approximation, if not sometimes actively misleading. Ware was presently in the domain of HUTGIN, ambassador in Italy, and had never before Black Easter had any need to invoke ASTAROTH or any of his inferior Intelligences. He was characterized by the *Grimorium Verum* as the Grand Duke of Hell, whereas Weirus referred to him as Grand Treasurer; while the *Grand Grimoire* did not mention him at all, assigning NEBIROS instead to an almost equivalent place. Nevertheless it seemed clear enough in general that while the domain of ASTAROTH might technically be in America, his principality was not confined thereto, but might make itself known anywhere in the world. HUTGIN in comparison was a considerably lesser figure.

And the war was not yet over, and Ware might indeed find some way to make himself useful; Baines had been right about that, too. But in what way remained unclear.

Very probably, he would have to go to Dis to find out. It was a terrifying thought, but Ware could see no way around it. That was where the center of power was now, where the war would henceforth be directed; and there, if Baines actually succeeded in reaching the SAC in Denver, Ware conceivably might succeed in arranging some sort of a *detente*. Certainly he would be of no use squatting here in ruined Italy, with all the superior spirits half a world away.

But how to get there? He did not have Baines's power to commandeer an aircraft, and though he was fully as wealthy as the industrialist—in fact most of the money had once been Baines's—it seemed wholly unlikely that any airline was selling tickets these days. A sea and overland journey would be too slow.

Would it be possible to compel ASTAROTH to provide him with some kind of an apport? This too was a terrifying thought. To the best of Ware's knowledge, the last magician to have ridden astride a devil had been Gerbert, back in the tenth century. He had resorted to it only to save his life from a predecessor of the Inquisition, whose attention he had amply earned; and, moreover, had lived through the ordeal to become Pope Sylvester II.

Gerbert had been a great man, and though Ware rather doubted that he had been any better a magician than Ware was, he did not feel prepared to try that conclusion just now. In any event, the process was probably unnecessarily drastic; transvection might serve the purpose just as well, or better. Though he had never been to a sabbat, he knew the theory and the particulars well enough. Included in the steel cabinets which held his magical pharmacopoeia were all the ingredients necessary for the flying ointment, and the compounding of it required no special time or ritual. As for piloting and navigation, that was to be sure a little alarming to anticipate, but if thousands upon thousands of ignorant old women had been able to fly a cleft stick, a distaff, a besom or even a shovel upon the first try, then so could Theron Ware.

First, however, he drew from the cabinet a flat slab of synthetic ruby, about the size and shape of an opened match folder; and from his cabinet of instruments, a burin. Upon the ruby, on the day of Mars, which is Tuesday, and in the hour of Mars, which is 0600, 1300, 2000 or 0300 on that day, he would engrave the following seal and characters:

This he would henceforth carry in his right shirt pocket like a reliquary. Though he would accept no help from ASTAROTH if he could possibly avoid it, it would be well, since he was going to be traveling in that fiend's domains, to be wearing his colors. As a purist, it bothered him a little that the ruby was synthetic, but his disturbance, he knew, was only an aesthetic one. ASTAROTH was a solar spirit, and the ancients, all the way through Albertus Magnus, had believed that rubies were engendered in the Earth by the influence of the Sun—but since they were not in fact formed that way, the persistence of the ruby in the ritual was only another example of one of the primary processes of magic, *superstition*, the gradual supremacy of the sign over the thing, so that so far as efficacy was concerned it did not matter a bit whether the ruby was synthetic or natural. Nature, too, obstinately refused to form rubies the size and shape of opened match folders.

For a magician, Ware reflected, there were indeed distinct advantages in being able to practice ten centuries after Gerbert had ridden upon his demon eagle.

VII

Transvection, too, has its hazards, Ware discovered. He crossed the Atlantic without incident in well under three hours—indeed, he suspected that in some aspect beyond the reach of his senses, the flight was taking place only partially in real time—and it began to look as though he would easily reach his goal before dawn. The candle affixed by its own tallow to the bundle of twigs and rushes before him (for only the foolhardy fly a broomstick with the brush trailing, no matter what is shown to the contrary in conventional Halloween cartoons) burned as steadily as though he were not in motion at all, casting a brilliant light ahead along his path; any ships at sea that might have seen him might have taken him to be an unusually brilliant meteor. As he approached the eastern United States, he wondered how he would show up on radar; the dropping of the bomb two days ago suggested that there might still be a number of functioning radomes there. In quieter times, he thought, he might perhaps have touched off another flying-saucer scare. Or was he visible at all? He discovered that he did not know, but he began to doubt it; the seaboard was hidden in an immense pall of smoke.

But once over land, he slowed himself down and lost altitude in order to get his bearings, and within what seemed to him to be only a very few minutes, he was grounded head over heels by the sound of a church bell forlornly calling what faithful might remain to midnight Mass. He remembered belatedly, when he got his wind back, that in some parts of Germany during the seventeenth-century flowering of the popular Goëtic cults, it had been the custom to toll church bells all night long as a protection against witches who might be passing overhead on the way to the Brocken; but the memory did him no good now—the besom had gone lifeless.

He had fallen in a rather mountainous, heavily timbered area, quite like the Harz Mountain section of Germany, but which he guessed to be somewhere in western Pennsylvania. Though it was now late April, which was doubtless warm in Positano, the night here was decidedly cold, especially for a thin man clad in nothing more than a light smear of unguent. He was instantly and violently all ashiver, for the sound of the bell had destroyed the protective as well as the transvective power of the flying ointment. He hastily undid the bundle of clothes, which was tied to the broomstick, but there were not going to be enough of them; after all, he had assembled them with Death Valley in mind. Also, he was beginning to feel drowsy and dizzy, and his pulse was blurred and banging with tachycardia. Among other things, the flying ointment contained both mandragora and belladonna, and now that the magic was gone out of it, these were exerting their inevitable side effects. He would have to wash the stuff off the minute he could find a stream, cold or no cold.

And not only because it was drugging him. Still other ingredients of the ointment were rather specifically organic in nature, and these gave it a characteristic smell which the heat of his body would gradually ripen. The chances were all too good that there would be some people in this country of the Amish—and not all of them old ones—who would know what that odor meant. Until he had had some kind of a bath, it would be dangerous even to ask for help.

Before dressing, he wiped off as much of it as he could with the towel in which the clothing had been tied. This he buried, together with the taper and the brush from the besom; and after making sure that the ruby talisman was still safely in his pocket, he set out, using the denuded broomstick as a staff.

The night-black, hilly, forested countryside would have made difficult going even for an experienced walker. Ware's life, on the other hand, had been nearly inactive except intellectually, and he was on the very near side of his fiftieth birthday. To his advantage, on the other hand, stood the fact that he had always been small and wiry, and the combination of a slightly hyperthyroid metabolism and an ascetic calling—he did not even smoke—had kept him that way, so that he made fair progress; and an equally lifelong love of descriptive astronomy, plus the necessity of astrology to his art, helped to keep him going in the right direction, whenever he could see a few stars through the smoke.

Just before dawn, he stumbled upon a small, rocky-bedded stream, and through the gloom heard the sound of a nearby waterfall. He moved against the current and shortly found this to be the spillway of a small log dam. Promptly he stripped and bathed under it, pronouncing in a whisper as he did so all three of the accompanying prayers from the rite of lustration as prescribed for the preparatory triduum in the *Grimorium Verum*—though the water was neither warm nor exorcised, it was obviously pure, and that would have to do.

The ablution was every bit as cold as he had expected it to be, and even colder was the process of air-drying himself; but he endured it stoically, for he had to get rid of what remained of the ointment, and moreover he knew that to put on damp clothes would be almost as dangerous. While he waited, his teeth chattering, faint traces of light began to appear through the trees from the east.

In answer, massive gray rectangular shapes began to sketch themselves against the darkness downstream, and before long he was able to see that to the west—which was the way the stream was momentarily running—the aisle it cut through the trees opened out onto a substantial farm. As if in confirmation of help to come, a cock crowed in the distance, a traditional ending for a night of magic.

But as the dawn continued to brighten, he saw that there would be no help for him here. Under the angle of the roof of the large barn nearest to him a circular diagram had been painted, like a formalized flower with an eye in it.

As Jack Ginsberg had taken the pains to find out long before he and his boss had even met the magician, Ware had been born and raised in the States and was still a citizen. As his name showed, his background was Methodist, but nevertheless he knew a hex sign when he saw one. And it gave him an idea.

He was not a witch, and he certainly had had no intention of laying a curse on this prosperous-looking farm ten seconds ago, but the opportunity to gather new data should not be missed.

Reaching into his shirt pocket, he turned the ruby around so that the seal and characters on it faced outward. In a low voice, he said, "THOMATOS, BENESSER, FLEANTER."

Under proper circumstances these words of the *Comte de Gabalis* encompassed the operator with thirty-three several Intelligences, but since the circumstances were not proper, Ware was not surprised when nothing happened. For one thing, his lustration had been imperfect; for another, he was using the wrong talisman—the infernal spirits of this ceremony were not devils but salamanders or fire elementals. Nevertheless he now added: "LITAN, ISER, OSNAS."

A morning breeze sprang up, and a leaflike whispering ran around him, which might or might not have been the voices of many beings individually saying, "NANTHER, NANTHER, NANTHER, NANTHER..." Touching the talisman, Ware said, "GITAU, HURANDOS, RIDAS, TALIMOL," and then, pointing to the barn, "UUSUR, ITAR."

The result should have been a highly localized but destructive earthquake, but there was not even a minor tremor, though he was pretty sure that he really had heard the responsive voices of the fire spirits. The spell simply would not work under the eye of the hex sign—one more piece of evidence that the powers of evil were still under some kind of restraint. That was good to know, but in a way, too, Ware was quite disappointed; for had he gotten his earthquake, the further words SOUTRAM, UBARSINENS would have compelled the Intelligences to carry him across the rest of his journey. He uttered them anyhow, but without result.

Neither in the *Comte de Gabalis* or its very late successor, *The Black Pullet*, did this ritual offer any word of dismissal, but nevertheless for safety's sake he now added: "RABIAM." Had this worked, he would have found himself carried home again, where at least he could have started over again with more ointment and another broomstick; but it did not. There was no recourse now but to seek out the farmhouse and try to persuade the farmer to give him something to eat and drive him to the nearest railhead. It was too bad that the man could not be told that he had just been protected by Ware from a demonic onslaught, but unfortunately the Amish did not believe that there was any such thing as white magic—and in the ultimate analysis they were quite right not to do so, whatever delusions about the point might be harbored by Father Domenico and his fellows.

Ware identified the farmhouse proper without any trouble. It looked every bit as clean, fat and prosperous as the rest, but it was suspiciously quiet; by this hour, everyone should be up and beginning the day's chores. He approached with caution, alert for guns or dogs, but the silence continued.

The caution had been needless. Inside, the place was an outright slaughterhouse, resembling nothing so much as the last act of Webster's *The White Devil*. Ware inspected it with clinical fascination. The family had been a large one—the parents, one grandparent, four daughters, three sons and the inevitable dog—and at some time during the preceding night they had suddenly fallen upon each other with teeth, nails, pokers, a buggy whip, a bicycle chain, a cleaver, a pig knife and the butt end of a smooth-bore musket, old enough to have been a relic of the Boer War. It was an obvious case of simultaneous mass possession, probably worked through the women, as these things almost always were. Doubtless they would infinitely have preferred a simple localized earthquake, but from an attack like this no conceivable peasant hex sign could have protected them.

Probably nothing could have, for as it had turned out, in their simple traditional religiosity they had chosen the wrong side. Like most of humankind, they had been born victims; even a beginning study of the Problem of Evil would have suggested to them that their God had never played fair with them, as indeed He had caused to be written out in Job for all to read; and their primitive backwoods demonology had never honestly admitted that there really were two sides to the Great Game, let alone allowing them any inkling of who the players were.

While he considered what to do next he prowled around the kitchen and the woodshed, where the larder was, trying not to slip or step on anybody. There were only two eggs—today's had obviously not been harvested—but he found smoked, streaky rashers of bacon, a day-old loaf of bread just ripe for cutting, nearly a pound of country butter and a stone jug of cold milk. All in all it was a good deal more than he could eat, but he built a fire in the old wood-burning stove, cooked the eggs and the bacon, and did his best to put it all down. After all, he had no idea when he would meet his next meal. He had already decided that he was not yet desperate enough to risk calling for an apport, but instead would keep walking generally westward until he met an opportunity to steal a car. (He would find none on the farm; the Amish still restricted themselves to horses.)

As he came out of the farmhouse into the bright morning, a sandwich in both hip pockets, he heard from the undestroyed barn a demanding lowing of cattle. Sorry, friends, he thought; nobody's going to milk you this morning.

VIII

Baines knew the structure and approaches of Strategic Air Command headquarters rather better than the Department of Defense would have thought right and proper even for a civilian with Q clearance, although there had been several people in DoD who would not have been at all surprised at it. The otherwise passengerless jet carrying him and Jack Ginsberg made no attempt to approach either Denver Airport or the U.S. Air Force Academy field at Colorado Springs, both of which, he correctly assumed, would no longer be in existence anyhow. Instead, he directed the pilot to land at Limon, a small town which was the easternmost vertex of a nearly equilateral triangle formed by these three points. Hidden there was one terminus of an underground rapid transit line which led directly into the heart of SAC's fortress—and was now its only surviving means of physical access to the outside world.

Baines and his secretary had been there only once before, and the guards at the station now were not only new but thoroughly frightened. Hence, despite the possession of ID cards countersigned by General McKnight, they were subjected to over an hour of questioning, fingerprinting, photographing of retinal blood-vessel patterns, frisking and fluoroscopy for hidden weapons or explosives, telephone calls into the interior and finally a closed-circuit television confrontation with McKnight himself before they were even allowed into the waiting room.

As if in partial compensation, the trip itself was rapid transit indeed. The line itself was a gravity-vacuum tube, bored in an exactly straight line under the curvature of the Earth, and kept as completely exhausted of air as out-gassing from its steel cladding would permit. The vacuum in the tube was in fact almost as hard as the atmosphere of the Moon. From the waiting room, Baines and Jack Ginsberg were passed through two airlocks into a seamlessly welded, windowless metal capsule which was sealed behind them. Here their guards strapped them in securely, for their own protection, for the initial kick of compressed air behind the capsule, abetted by rings of electromagnets, gave it an acceleration of more than five miles per hour per second. Though this is not much more than they might have been subjected to in an electric streetcar of about 1940, it is a considerable jerk if you cannot see outside and have nothing to hold on to. Thereafter, the capsule was simply allowed to fall to the mathematical midpoint of its right of way, gaining speed at about twenty-eight feet per second; since the rest of the journey was uphill, the capsule was slowed in proportion by gravity, friction and the compression of the almost nonexistent gases in the tube still ahead of it, which without any extra braking whatsoever brought it to a stop at the SAC terminus of the line so precisely that only a love pat from a fifteen horsepower engine was needed to line up its airlock with that of the station.

"When you're riding a thing like this, it makes it hard to believe that there's any such thing as a devil, doesn't it?" Jack Ginsberg said. He had had a long, luxurious shower aboard the plane, and that, plus getting away from the demon-haunted ruins in Positano, and the subsequent finding in Zurich that money still worked, had brightened him perceptibly.

"Maybe," Baines said. "A large part of the mystic tradition says that the possession and use of secular knowledge—or even the desire for it—is in itself evil, according to Ware. But here we are."

But in the smooth-running, even-temperatured caverns of the SAC, Baines himself felt rather reassured. There was no Goat grinning over his shoulder yet. McKnight was an old friend; he was pleased to see Buelg again, and honored to meet Šatvje; and down here, at least, everything seemed to be under control. It was also helpful to find that both McKnight and his advisers not only already knew the real situation, but had very nearly accepted it. Only Buelg had remained a little skeptical at the beginning, and had seemed quite taken aback to find Baines, of all people, providing independent testimony to the same effect as had the computer. When the new facts Baines had brought had been fed into the machine, and the machine had produced in response a whole new batch of conclusions entirely consistent with the original hypothesis, Buelg seemed convinced, although it was plain that he still did not like it. Well, who did?

At long last they were comfortably settled in McKnight's office, with three tumblers of Jack Daniel's (Jack Ginsberg did not drink, and neither did Šatvje) and no one to interrupt them but an occasional runner from Chief Hay. Though the runner was a coolly pretty blond girl, and the USAF's women's auxiliary had apparently adopted the miniskirt, Ginsberg did not seem to notice. Perhaps he was still in shock from his recent run-in with the succubus. To Baines's eyes, the girl did look rather remarkably like Ware's Greta, which should have captured Jack instantly; but then, in the long run, most women looked alike to Baines, especially in the line of business.

"That bomb did you no good at all, I take it," he said.

"Oh, I wouldn't go so far as to say that," McKnight said. "True, it didn't destroy the city, or even hurt it visibly, but it certainly seemed to take them by surprise. For about an hour after the fireball went up, the sky above the target was full of them. It was like firing a flashbulb in a cave full of sleeping bats—and we got pictures, too."

"Any evidence that you, uh, destroyed any of them?"

"Well, we saw a lot of them going back to the city under their own power—despite very bad design, they seem to fly pretty well—but we don't have any count of how many went up. We didn't see any falling, but that might have been because some of them had been vaporized."

"Not bloody likely. Their bodies may have been vaporized, but the bodies were borrowed in the first place. Like knocking down a radio-controlled aircraft: the craft may be a total loss, but the controlling Intelligence is unharmed, somewhere else, and can send another one against you whenever it likes."

"Excuse me, Doctor Baines, but the analogy is inexact," Buelg said. "We know that because we did get a lot out of the bomb besides simply stirring up a flurry. High-speed movies of the column of the mushroom as it went up show a lot of the creatures trying to reform. One individual we were able to follow went through thirty-two changes in the first minute. The changes are all incredible and beyond any physical theory or model we can erect to account for them, but they do show, first, that the creature was seriously inconvenienced, and second, that it wanted and perhaps needed to hold onto *some* kind of physical form. That's a start. It suggests to me that had we been able to confine them all in the fireball, where the temperatures are way higher still, no gamut of change they could have run through would have done them any good. Eventually they would have been stripped of the last form and utterly destroyed."

"The last form, maybe," Baines said. "But the spirit would remain. I don't know why they're clinging to physical forms so determinedly, but it probably has only a local and tactical reason, something to do with the prosecuting of the present war. But you can't destroy a spirit by such means, any more than you can destroy a message by burning the piece of paper it's written on."

As he said this, he became uncomfortably aware that he had gotten the argument out of some sermon against atheism that he had heard as a boy, and had thought simple-minded even then. But since then, he had *seen* demons—and a lot more closely than anybody else here had.

"That is perhaps an open question," Šatvje said heavily. "I am not myself a skeptic, you should understand, Doctor Baines, but I have to remind myself that no spirit has ever been so intensively tested to destruction before. Inside a thermonuclear fireball, even the nuclei of hydrogen atoms find it difficult to retain their integrity."

"Atomic nuclei remain matter, and the conservation laws still apply. Demons are neither matter nor energy; they are something else."

"We do not know that they are not energy," Šatvje said. "They may well be fields, falling somewhere within the electro-magnetico-gravitic triad. Remember that we have never achieved a unified field theory; even Einstein repudiated his in the last years of his life, and quantum mechanics—with all respect to De Broglie—is only a clumsy avoidance of the problem. These ... spirits ... may be such unified fields. And one characteristic of such fields might be 100 percent negative entropy."

"There couldn't be any such thing as completely negative entropy," Buelg put in. "Such a system would constantly *accumulate* order, which means that it would run backward in time and we would never be aware of it at all. You have to allow for Planck's Constant. This would be the only stable case—"

He wrote rapidly on a pad, stripped off the sheet and passed it across the table. The note read, in very neat lettering:

$$H(x) - H_y(x) = C + \epsilon$$

The girl came in with another manifold of sheets from the computer, and this time Jack Ginsberg's eye could be observed to be wandering haunchward a little. Baines had never objected to this—he preferred his most valuable employees to have a few visible and usable weaknesses—but for once he almost even sympathized; he was feeling a little out of his depth.

"Meaning what?" he said.

"Why," Šatvje said, a little patronizingly, "eternal life, of course.

Life *is* negative entropy. Stable negative entropy is eternal life."

"Barring accidents," Buelg said, with a certain grim relish. "We have no access yet to the gravitic part of the spectrum, but the electromagnetic sides are totally vulnerable, and with the clues we've got now, we ought to be able to burst into such a closed system like a railroad spike going through an auto tire."

"If you can kill a demon," Baines said slowly, "then—"

"That's right," Buelg said affably. "Angel, devil, ordinary immortal soul—you name it, we can do for it. Not right away, maybe, but before very long."

"Perhaps the ultimate human achievement," Šatvje said, with a dreaming, almost beatific expression. "The theologians call condemnation to Hell the Second Death. Soon, perhaps, we may be in a position to give the Third Death ... the bliss of complete extinction ... liberation from the Wheel!"

McKnight's eyes were now also wandering, though toward the ceiling. He wore the expression of a man who has heard all this before, and is not enjoying it any better the second time. Baines himself was very far from being bored—indeed, he was as close to horrified fascination as he had ever been in his life—but clearly it was time to bring everybody back to Earth. He said:

"Talk's cheap. Do you have any actual plans?"

"You bet we do," McKnight said, suddenly galvanized. "I've had Chief Hay run me an inventory of the country's remaining military power, and, believe me, there's a lot of it. I was surprised myself. We are going to mount a major attack upon this city of Dis, and for it we're going to bring some things up out of the ground that the American people have never seen before and neither has anybody else, including this pack of demons. I don't know why they're just sitting there, but maybe it's because they think they've already got us licked. Well, they're dead wrong. Nobody can lick the United States—not in the long run!"

It was an extraordinary sentiment from a man who had been maintaining for years that the United States had "lost" China, "surrendered" Korea, "abandoned" Vietnam and was overrun by home-bred Communists; but Baines, who knew the breed, saw no purpose in calling attention to the fact. *Their arguments, not being based in reason, cannot be swayed by reason.* Instead he said:

"General, believe me, I advise against it. I know some of the weapons you're talking about, and they're pretty powerful. I ought to know; my company designed and supplied some of them, so it would be against my own interests to run them down to you. But I very much doubt that any of them will do any good under the present circumstances."

"That, of course, remains to be seen," McKnight said.

"I'd rather we didn't. If they work, we may find ourselves worse off than before. That's the point I came here to press. The demons are about 90 percent in charge of the world now, but you'll notice that they haven't taken any further steps against us. There's a reason for this. They are fighting against another Opponent entirely, and it's quite possible that we ought to be on their side."

McKnight leaned back in his chair, with the expression of a president confronted at a press conference with a question on which he had not been briefed.

"Let me be quite sure I understand you, Doctor Baines," he said. "Do you propose that the present invasion of the United States was a good thing? And, further, that we ought not to be opposing the occupying forces with all our might? That indeed we ought instead to be aiding and abetting the powers responsible for it?"

"I don't propose any aiding and abetting whatsoever," Baines said, with an inward sigh. "I just think we ought to lay off for a while, that's all, until we see how the situation works out."

"You are almost the last man in the world," McKnight said stiffly, "whom I would have suspected of being a ComSymp, let alone a pro-Chink. When I have your advice entered upon the record, I will also add an expression of my personal confidence. In the meantime, the attack goes forward as scheduled."

Baines said nothing more, advisedly. It had occurred to him, out of his experience with Theron Ware, that angels fallen and unfallen, and the immortal part of man, partook of and had sprung from the essentially indivisible nature of their Creator; that if these men could destroy that Part, they could equally well dissolve the Whole; that a successful storming of Dis would inevitably be followed by a successful war upon Heaven; and that if God were not dead yet, He soon might be.

However it turned out, it looked like it was going to be the most interesting civil war he had ever run guns to.

IX

UNITED STATES ARMED FORCES
Strategic Air Command Office
Denver, Colorado

Date: May 1

MEMORANDUM: Number I
TO: All Combat Arms
SUBJECT: General Combat Orders

1. This Memorandum supersedes all previous directives on this subject.
2. The United States has been invaded and all combat units will stand in readiness to expel the invading forces.
3. The enemy has introduced a number of combat innovations of which all units must be made thoroughly aware. All officers will therefore read this Memorandum in full to their respective commands, and will thereafter post it in a conspicuous place. All commands should be sampled for familiarity with the contents of the Memorandum.
4. Enemy troops are equipped with individual body armor. In accordance with ancient Oriental custom, this armor has been designed and decorated in various grotesque shapes, in the hope of frightening the opposition. It is expected that the American soldier

will simply laugh at this primitive device. All personnel are warned, however, that as armor these "demon suits" are extremely effective. A very high standard of marksmanship will be required against them.

5. An unknown number of the enemy body armor units, perhaps approaching 100%, are capable of free flight, like the jump suits supplied to U.S. Mobile Infantry. Ground forces will therefore be alert to possible attack from the air by individual enemy troops as well as by conventional aircraft.

6. It is anticipated that in combat the enemy will employ various explosive, chemical and toxic agents which may produce widespread novel effects. All personnel are hereby reminded that these effects will be either natural in origin, or illusions.

7. Following the reading of this Memorandum, all officers will read to their commands those paragraphs of the Articles of War pertaining to the penalties for cowardice in battle.

By order of the Commander in Chief:

D. Willis McKnight

D. WILLIS MCKNIGHT
General of the Armies, USAF

Because of the destruction of Rome and of the Vatican with it—alas for that great library and treasure house of all Christendom!—the Holy See had been moved to Venice, which had been spared thus far, and was now housed in almost equal magnificence in the Sala del Collegio of the Palazzo Ducale, the only room to escape intact from the great fire of 1577, where, under a ceiling by Veronese, the doges had been accustomed to receive their ambassadors to other city-states. It was the first time the palace had been used by anybody but tourists since Napoleon had forced the abdication of Lodovico Manin exactly eleven hundred years after the election of the first doge.

There were no tourists here now, of course; the city, broiling hot and stinking of the garbage in its canals, brooded lifelessly under the Adriatic sun, a forgotten museum. Nobody was about in the crazy narrow streets and the cramped *ristoranti* but the native Venetians, their livelihood gone, sullenly starving together in small groups and occasionally snarling at each other in their peculiar dialect. Many already showed signs of radiation sickness: their hair was shedding in patches, and pools of vomit caught the sunlight, ignored by everyone but the flies.

The near desertion of the city, at least by comparison with the jam which would have been its natural state by this time of year, gave Father Domenico a small advantage. Instead of having to take refuge in a third-class hotel, clamorous twenty-four hours a day with groups of Germans and Americans being processed by the coachload like raw potatoes being converted into neatly packaged crisps, he was able without opposition to find himself apartments in the Patriarch's Palace itself. Such dusty sumptuousness did not at all suit him, but he had come to see the Pope, as the deputy of an ancient, still honored monastic order; and the Patriarch, after confessing him and hearing the nature of his errand, had deemed it fitting that he be appropriately housed while he waited.

There was no way of telling how long the wait might be. The Pope had died with Rome; what remained of the College of Cardinals—those of them that had been able to reach Venice at all—was shut in the Sala del Consiglio dei Dieci, attempting to elect a new one. It was said that the office of the Grand Inquisitor, directly next door, held a special guest, but of this rumor the Patriarch seemed to know no more than the next man. In the meantime, he issued to Father Domenico a special dispensation to conduct Masses and hear confessions in several small churches off the Grand Canal, and to preach there and even in the streets if he wished. Technically, Father Domenico had no patent to do any of these things, since he was a monk rather than a priest, but the Patriarch, like everyone else now, was short on manpower.

On the trip northward from Monte Albano, Father Domenico had seen many more signs of suffering, and of outright demoniac malignancy, than were visible on the surface of this uglily beautiful city; but it was nevertheless a difficult, almost sinister place in which to attempt to minister to the people, let alone to preach a theology of hope. The Venetians had never been more than formally and outwardly allegiant to the Church from at least their second treaty with Islam in the mid-fifteenth century. The highest pinnacle of their ethics was that of dealing fairly with each other, and since there was at the same time no sweeter music to Venetian ears than the scream of outrage from the outsider who had discovered too late that he had been cheated, this left them little that they felt they ought to say in the confessional. Most of them seemed to regard the now obvious downfall of almost all of human civilization as a plot to divert the tourist trade to some other town—probably Istanbul, which they still referred to as Constantinople.

As for hope, they had none. In this they were not alone. Throughout his journey, Father Domenico had found nothing but terror and misery, and a haunted populace which could not but conclude that everything the Church had taught them for nearly two thousand years had been lies. How could he tell them that, considering the real situation as he knew it to be, the suffering and the evil with which they were afflicted were rather less than he had expected to find? How then could he tell them further that he saw small but mysteriously increasing signs of mitigation of the demons' rule? In these, fighting all the way against confounding hope with wishful thinking, he believed only reluctantly himself.

Yet hope somehow found its way forward. On an oppressive afternoon while he was trying to preach to a group of young thugs, most of them too surly and indifferent even to jeer, before the little Church of Sta. Maria dei Miracoli, his audience was suddenly galvanized by a series of distant whistles. The whistles, as Father Domenico knew well enough, had been until only recently the signals of the young wolves of Venice, to report the spotting of some escortless English schoolmarm, pony-tailed Bennington art student or gaggle of Swedish girls. There were no such prey about now, but nevertheless, the piazzetta emptied within a minute.

Bewildered and of course apprehensive, Father Domenico followed, and soon found the streets almost as crowded as of old with people making for St. Mark's. A rumor had gone around that a puff of white smoke had been seen over the Palazzo Ducale. This was highly unlikely, since—what with the fear of another fire which constantly haunted the palace—there was no stove in it anywhere in which to burn ballots; nevertheless, the expectation of a new Pope had run through the city like fire itself. By the time Father Domenico reached the vast square opposite the basilica (for after all, he too had come in search of a Pope) it was so crowded as to scarcely leave standing room for the pigeons.

If there was indeed to be any announcement, it would have to come Venetian style from the top of the Giant's Staircase of Antonio Rizzo; the repetitive arches of the first-floor loggia offered no single balcony on which a Pope might appear. Father Domenico pressed forward into the great internal courtyard toward the staircase, at first saying, *"Prego, prego,"* and then *"Scusate, scusate mi,"* to no effect whatsoever, and finally with considerable judicious but hard monkish use of elbows and knees.

Over the tense rumbling of the crowd there sounded suddenly an antiphonal braying of many trumpets—something of Gabrielli's, no doubt—and at the same time Father Domenico found himself jammed immovably against the coping of the cannonfounder's well, which had long since been scavenged clean of the tourists' coins. By luck it was not a bad position; from here he had quite a clear view up the staircase and between the towering statues of Mars and Neptune. The great doors had already been opened, and the cardinals in their scarlet finery were ranked on either side of the portico. Between them and a little forward stood two pages, one of them holding a red cushion upon which stood something tall and glittering.

Amidst the fanfare, an immensely heavy tolling began to boom: La Trottiera, the bell which had once summoned the members of the Grand Council to mount their horses and ride over the wooden bridges to a meeting. The combination of bell and trumpets was solemnly beautiful, and under it the crowd fell quickly silent. Yet the difference from the Roman ritual was disturbing, and there was something else wrong about it, too. What was that thing on the cushion? It certainly could not be the tiara; was it the golden horn of the doges?

The music and the tolling stopped. Into the pigeon-cooing silence, a cardinal cried in Latin:

"We have a Pope, *Summus Antistitum Antistes!* And it is his will that he be called Juvenember LXIX!"

The unencumbered page now stepped forward. He called in the vernacular:

"Here is your Pope, and we know it will please you."

From the shadow of the great doors, there stepped forth into the sunlight between the statues, bowing his head to accept the golden horn, his face white and mild as milk, the special guest of the office of the Grand Inquisitor: a comely old man with a goshawk on his wrist, whom Father Domenico had first and last seen on Black Easter, released from the Pit by Theron Ware—the demon AGARES.

There was an enormous shout from the crowd, and then the trumpets and the bell resumed, now joined by all the rest of the bells in the city, and by many drums, and the firing of cannon. Choking with horror, Father Domenico fled as best he could.

The festival went on all week, climaxed by bull dancing in the Cretan style in the courtyard of the Palazzo, and by fireworks at night, while Father Domenico prayed. This event was definitive. The Antichrist had arrived, however belatedly, and therefore God still lived. Father Domenico could do no more good in Italy; he must now go to Dis, into Hell-mouth itself, and challenge Satan to grant His continuing existence. Nor would it be enough for Father Domenico to aspire to be the Antisatan. If necessary—most terrifying of all thoughts—he must now expose himself to the temptation and the election, by no Earthly college, of becoming the vicar of Christ whose duty it would be to harrow this Earthly Hell.

Yet how to get there? He was isolated on an isthmus of mud, and he had no Earthly resources whatsoever. Just possibly, some rite of white magic might serve to carry him, although he could remember none that seemed applicable; but that would involve returning to Monte Albano, and in any event, he felt instinctively that no magic of any kind would be appropriate now.

In this extremity, he bethought him of certain legends and attested miracles of the early saints, some of whom in their exaltation were said to have been lifted long distances through the air. Beyond question, he was not a saint; but if his forthcoming role was to be as he suspected, some similar help might be vouchsafed him. He tried to keep his mind turned away from the obvious and most exalted example of all, and equally to avoid thinking about the doubt-inducing fate of Simon Magus—a razor's edge which not even his Dominican training made less than nearly impossible to negotiate.

Nevertheless, his shoulders squared, his face set, Father Domenico walked resolutely toward the water.

X

Even after the complete failure of air power in Vietnam to pound one half of a tenth-rate power into submission, General McKnight remained a believer in its supremacy; but he was not such a fool as to do without ground support, knowing very well the elementary rule that territory must be occupied as well as devastated, or even the most decisive victory will come unstuck. By the day—or rather, the night—for which the attack was scheduled, he had moved three armored divisions into the Panamint range, and had two more distributed through the Grapevine, Funeral and Black mountains, which also bristled with rocket emplacements. This was by no means either as big or as well divided a force as he should have liked to have used, especially on the east, but since it was all the country had left to offer him, he had to make it do.

His battle plan was divided into three phases. Remembering that the test bomb had blown some thousands of enemy troops literally sky high for what was tactically speaking quite a long period of time, he intended to begin with a serial bombardment of Dis with as many of his remaining nuclear weapons as he could use up just short of making the surrounding territory radiologically lethal to his own men. These warheads might not do the city or the demons any damage—a proposition which he still regarded with some incredulity—but if they would again disorganize the enemy and keep him from reforming, that would be no mean advantage in itself.

Phase Two was designed to take advantage of the fact that the battleground from his point of view was all downhill, the devils with stunning disregard of elementary strategy having located their fortress at the lowest point in the valley, on the site of what had previously been Badwater, which was actually two hundred and eighty-two feet below sea level. When the nuclear bombardment ended, it would be succeeded immediately by a continued hammering with conventional explosives, by artillery, missiles and planes. These would include phosphorus bombs, again probably harmless to devils, but which would in any event produce immense clouds of dense white smoke, which might impair visibility for the enemy; his own troops could see through it handily enough by radar, and would always be able to see the main target through the infrared telescope or "sniperscope," since even under normal conditions it was always obligingly kept red hot. Under cover of this bombardment, McKnight planned a rush of armor upon the city, spearheaded by halftrack-mounted laser projectors. It was McKnight's theory, supported neither by his civilian advisers nor by the computer, that the thermonuclear fireball had failed to vaporize the iron walls because its heat had been too generalized and diffuse, and that the concentrated heat of four or five or a dozen laser beams, all focused on one spot, might punch its way through like a rapier going through cheese. This onslaught was to be aimed directly at the gates. Of course these would be better defended than any other part of the perimeter, but a significant number of the defenders might still be flapping wildly around in the air amidst the smoke, and in any event, when one is trying to breach a wall, it is only common sense to begin at a point which *already* has a hole in it.

If such a breach was actually effected, an attempt would be made to enlarge it with land torpedoes, particularly burrowing ones of the Hess type which would have been started on their way at the beginning of Phase One. These had never seen use before in actual combat and were supposed to be graveyard secret—though with the profusion of spies and traitors with which America had been swarming, in McKnight's view, before all this had begun, he doubted that the secret had been very well kept. (After all, if even Baines ...) He was curious also about the actual effectiveness of another secret, the product of an almost incestuous union of chemistry and nucleonics called TDX, a compound as unstable as TNT, which was made of gravity-polarized atoms. McKnight had only the vaguest idea of what this jargon was supposed to signify, but what he did know was its action; TDX was supposed to have the property of exploding in a flat plane, instead of expanding evenly in all directions like any Christian explosive.

Were the gate forced, the bombardment would stop and Phase Three would follow. This would be an infantry assault, supported by individually airborne troops in their rocket-powered flying harness, and supplemented by an attempted paratroop landing inside the city. If on the other hand the gate did not go down, there would be a most unwelcome Phase Four—a general, and hopefully orderly retreat.

The whole operation could be watched both safely and conveniently from the SAC's Command Room under Denver, and as the name implied, directed in the same way; there was a multitude of television screens, some of which were at the individual command consoles provided for each participating general. The whole complex closely resembled the now extinct Space Center at Houston, which had in fact been modeled after it; technically, space flight and modern warfare are almost identical operations from the command point of view. At the front of this cavern and quite dominating it was a master screen of Cinerama proportions; at its rear was something very like a sponsors' booth, giving McKnight and his guests an overview of the whole, as well as access to a bank of small screens on which he could call into being any individual detail of the action that was within access of a camera.

McKnight did not bother to occupy the booth until the nuclear bombardment was over, knowing well enough that the immense amount of ionization it would produce would make non-cable television reception impossible for quite some time. (The fallout was going to be hell, too—but almost all of it would miss Denver, the East Coast was dead, and the fish and the Europeans would have to look out for themselves.) When he finally took over, the conventional bombardment was just beginning. With him were Baines, Buelg, Chief Hay and Šatvje; Jack Ginsberg had expressed no particular interest in watching, and since Baines did not need him here, he had been excused to go below, presumably to resume his lubricious pursuit of Chief Hay's comely runner.

Vision on the great master screen was just beginning to clear as they took their seats, although there was still considerable static. Weather Control reported that it was a clear, brightly moonlit night over all of the Southwest, but in point of fact the top of the great multiple nuclear mushroom, shot through with constant lightning, now completely covered the southern third of California and all of the two states immediately to the east of it. The units and crews crouching in their bivouacs and emplacements along the sides of the mountains facing away from the valley clung grimly to the rocks against hurricane updrafts in temperatures that began at a hundred and fifty degrees and went on up from there. No unit which had been staked out on any of the inside faces of any of the ranges reported anything, then or ever; even the first missiles and shells to come screaming in toward Dis exploded incontinently in midair the moment they rose above the sheltering shadows of the mountain peaks. No thermocouple existed which would express in degrees the temperature at the heart of the target itself; spectrographs taken from the air showed it to be cooling from a level of about two and a half million electron volts, a figure as utterly impossible to relate to human experience as are the distances in miles between the stars.

Nevertheless, the valley cooled with astonishing rapidity, and once visibility was restored, it was easy to see why. More than two hundred square miles of it had been baked and annealed into a shallow, even dish, still glowing whitely but shot through with the gorgeous colors of impurities, like a borax bead in the flame of a blowpipe; and this was acting like the reflector of a searchlight, throwing the heat outward through the atmosphere into space in an almost solidly visible column. At its center, as at the Cassegranian focus of a telescope mirror, was a circular black hole.

McKnight leaned forward, grasping the arms of his chair in a death grip, and shouted for a close-up. Had the job been done already? Perhaps Buelg had been right about there being a possible limit to the number of transformations the enemy could go through before final dissolution. After all, Badwater had just received a nuclear saturation which had previously been contemplated only in terms of the overkill of whole countries—

But as the glass darkened, the citadel brightened, until at last it showed once more as a red-hot ring. Nothing could be seen inside it but a roiling mass of explosions—the conventional bombardment was now getting home, and with great accuracy—from which a mushroom stem continued to rise in the very center of the millennial updraft; but the walls—the walls, the walls, the walls were still there.

"Give it up, General," Buelg said, his voice gravelly. "No matter what the spectroscope shows, if those walls were really iron—" He paused and swallowed heavily. "They must be only symbologically iron, perhaps in some alchemical sense. Otherwise the atoms would not only have been scattered to the four winds, but would have had all the electron shells stripped off them. You can do nothing more but lose more lives."

"The bombardment is still going on," McKnight pointed out

stiffly, "and we've had no report yet of what it's done to the enemy's organization and manpower. For all we know, there's nobody left down that hole at all—and the laser squadrons haven't even arrived yet, let alone the Hess torpedoes."

"Neither of which are going to work worth a damn," Baines said brutally. "I know what the Hess torpedo will do. Have you forgotten that they were invented by my own chief scientist? Who just incidentally was taken by PUT SATANACHIA this Easter, so that the demons now know all about the gadget, if they didn't before. And after what's been dropped on that town already, expecting anything of it is like trying to kill a dinosaur by kissing it."

"It is in the American tradition," McKnight said, "to do things the hard way if there is no other way. Phase Four is a last-ditch measure, and it is good generalship—which I do not expect you to understand—to remain flexible until the last moment. As Clausewitz remarks, most battles are lost by generals who failed to have the courage of their own convictions in the clutch."

Baines, who had read extensively in both military and political theoreticians in five languages, and had sampled them in several more, as a necessary adjunct to his business, knew very well that Clausewitz had never said any such damn fool thing, and that McKnight was only covering with an invented quotation a hope which was last-ditch indeed. But even had elementary Machiavellianism given him any reason to suppose that charging McKnight with this would change the General's mind in the slightest, he could see from the master screen that it was already too late. While they had been talking, the armored divisions had been charging down into the valley, their diesel-electric engines snarling and snorting, the cleats of their treads cracking the slippery glass and leaving sluggishly glowing, still quasi-molten trails behind. Watching them in the small screens, Baines began to think that he must be wrong. He knew these monsters well—they were part of his stock in trade—and to believe that they were resistible went against the selling habits of an entire adult lifetime.

Yet some of them were bogging down already; as they descended deeper into the valley, with the small rockets whistling over their hunched heads, the hot glass under their treads worked into the joints like glue, and then, carried by the groaning engines up over the top trunnions, cooled and fell into the bearings in a shower of many-sized abrasive granules. The monsters slewed and sidled, losing traction and with it, steerage; and then the lead half-track with the laser cannon jammed immovably and began to sink like the *Titanic* into the glass, the screams of its broiling crew tearing the cool air of the command booth like a ripsaw until McKnight impatiently cut the sound off.

The other beasts lumbered on regardless—they had no orders to do otherwise—and a view from the air showed that three or four units of the laser squadron were now within striking distance of the gates of Dis. Like driver ants, black streams of infantry were crawling down the inner sides of the mountains behind the last wave of the armored divisions. They too had had no orders to turn back. Even in their immensely clumsy asbestos firemen's suits and helmets, they were already fainting and falling over each other in the foothills, their carefully oiled automatic weapons falling into the sand, the tanks of their flame throwers splitting and dumping jellied gasoline on the hot rocks, the very air of the valley sucking all of the moisture out of their lungs through the tiniest cracks in their uniforms.

Baines was not easily horrified—that would have been bad for business—but also he had never before seen any actual combat but the snippets of the Vietnam War, which had been shown on American television. This senseless advance of expensively trained and equipped men to certain and complete slaughter—men who as usual not only had no idea of what they were dying for, but had been actively misled about it—made about as much military sense as the Siege of Sevastopol or the Battle of the Marne. Certainly it was spectacular, but intellectually it was not even very interesting.

Four of the laser buggies—all that had survived—were now halted before the gates, two to each side to allow a heavy howitzer to fire between them. From them lanced out four pencil-thin beams of intensely pure red light, all of which met at the same spot on the almost invisible seam between the glowing doors. Had that barrier been real iron, they would have holed through it in a matter of seconds in a tremendous shower of sparks, but in actuality they were not even raising its temperature, as far as Baines could see. The beams winked out; then struck again.

Above the buggies, on the barbican, there seemed to be scores of black, indistinct, misshapen figures. They were very active, but their action did not seem to be directed against the buggies; Baines had the mad impression, which he was afraid was all too accurate, that they were dancing.

Again the beams lashed out. Beside him, McKnight muttered:

"If they don't hurry it up—"

Even before he was able to finish the sentence, the ground in front of the gates erupted. The first of the Hess torpedoes had arrived. One of the half-tracks simply vanished, while the one next to it went slowly skyward, and as slowly fell back, in a fountain of armor plate, small parts, and human limbs and torsos. Another, on the very edge of the crater, toppled equally slowly into it. The fourth sat for a long minute as if stunned by the concussion, and then began to back slowly away.

Another torpedo went off directly under the gates, and then another. The gates remained obdurately unharmed, but after a fourth such blast, light could be seen under them—the crater was growing.

"Halt all armored vehicles!" McKnight shouted into his intercom, pounding the arm of his chair in excitement. "Infantry advance on the double! We're going under!"

Another Hess torpedo went off in the same gap. Baines was fascinated now, and even feeling a faint glow of pride. Really, the things worked very well indeed; too bad Hess couldn't be here to see it ... but maybe he was seeing it, from inside. That hole was already big enough to accommodate a small car, and while he watched, another torpedo blew it still wider and deeper.

"Paratroops! Advance drop by ten minutes!"

But why was Hess's invention working when the nuclear devices hadn't? Maybe Dis had only sunk lower as a whole, as the desert around and beneath it had been vaporized, but the demons could not defend the purely mundane geology of the valley itself? Another explosion. How many of those torpedoes had the Corps of Engineers had available? Consolidated Warfare Service had supplied only ten prototypes with the plans at the time of the sale, and there hadn't been time to put more into production. McKnight's suddenly advanced timetable seemed nevertheless to be allowing for the arrival of all ten.

This proved to be the case, except that the ninth got caught in a fault before it had completed its burrowing and blew up in the middle of one of the advancing columns of troops. Hess had always frankly admitted that the machine would be subject to this kind of failure, and that the flaw was inherent in the principle rather than the design. But it probably wouldn't be missed; the gap under the gates of Dis now looked quite as big as the New Jersey entrance to the original two Lincoln Tunnels. And the infantry was arriving at speed.

And at that moment, the vast unscarred gates slowly began to swing inward. McKnight gaped in astonishment, and Baines could feel his own jaw dropping. Was the citadel going to surrender before it had even been properly stormed? Or worse, had it been ready all along to open to the first polite knock, so that all this colossal and bloody effort had been unnecessary?

But that, at least, they were spared. As the first patrols charged, tumbled, scrambled and clambered into the crater, there appeared in the now fully opened gateway, silhouetted against the murky flames behind, the same three huge naked snaky-haired women that McKnight and his crew had seen in the very first aerial photographs. They were all three carrying among them what appeared to be the head of an immense decapitated statue of something much like one of themselves. The asbestos-clad soldiers climbing up the far wall of the crater could not turn any grayer than they were, but they froze instantaneously like the overwhelmed inhabitants of

Pompeii, and fell, and as they fell, they broke. Within minutes, the pit was being refilled from the bottom with shattered sculpture.

Overhead, the plane carrying the first contingent of paratroops was suddenly blurred by hundreds of tiny black dots. Seconds later, the fuselage alone was plunging toward the desert; the legions of BEELZEBUB, the Lord of the Flies, had torn the wings off men. Lower, in the middle of the air, rocket-borne Assault Infantry soldiers were being plucked first of their harness, then of their clothing, and then of their hair, their fingernails and toenails by jeering creatures with beasts' heads, most of whom were flying without even wings. The bodies, when there was anything left of them at all, were being dropped unerringly into the heart of the Pit.

In summary, the Siege of Dis could more reasonably be described as a rout, except for one curious discrepancy: When Phase Four began—without anyone's ordering it, and otherwise not according to plan—the demons failed to follow up their advantage. None of them, in fact, had ever left the city; even when they had taken to the air, they had never crossed its perimeter, as though the moat represented some absolute boundary which ascended even into the sky.

But the slaughter had been bad enough already. The chances that the Army of the United States could ever reform again looked very small indeed.

And at the end, there formed upon the master screen in the Denver cavern, superimposed upon the image of the burning, triumphant city, an immense Face. Baines knew it well; he had been expecting to see it again ever since the end of that Black Easter back in Positano.

It was the crowned goat's head of PUT SATANACHIA.

McKnight gasped in horror for the very first time in Baines's memory; and down on the floor of the control center, several generals fainted outright at their consoles. Then McKnight was on his feet, screaming.

"A Chink! I knew it all along! Hay, clear the circuits! Clear the circuits! Get him off the screen!" He rounded suddenly on Baines.

"And you, you traitor! Your equipment failed us! You've sold us out! You were on their side all the time! Do you know into whose hands you have delivered your country? Do you? Do you?"

His howling was only an irritant now, but Baines had the strength left to raise one mocking eyebrow questioningly. McKnight leveled a trembling finger at the screen.

"Hay, Hay, clear the circuits! I'll have you court-martialed! Doesn't anyone understand but me? *That is the insidious Doctor Fu Manchu!*"

The Sabbath Goat paid him no heed. Instead, it looked directly and steadily across the cavern into Baines's eyes. There was no mistaking the direction of that regard, and no question but that it saw him. It said:

Ah, there you are, my dearly beloved son. Come to me now. Our Father Below hath need of thee.

Baines had no intention whatsoever of obeying that summons; but he found himself rising from his chair all the same.

Foaming at the mouth, his hands clawing for the distant throat of the demon, McKnight plunged in a shower of splinters through the front of the booth and fell like a glass comet toward the floor.

The Harrowing of Heaven

As a picture, wherein a black coloring occurs in its proper place, so is the universe beautiful, if any could survey it, notwithstanding the presence of sinners, although, taken by themselves, their proper deformity makes them hideous.
—St. Augustine: *De Civitate Dei*, xi. 23

Thus that Faustus, to so many a snare of death, had now, neither willing nor witting it, begun to loosen that wherein I was taken.
—*Confessions*, v. 13

XI

Baines did not have much time to experiment under the geas or compulsion which PUT SATANACHIA had laid upon him, but he nevertheless found that it was highly selective in character. For example, the great prince had said nothing about requiring the presence of Jack Ginsberg, but when Baines, in a mixture of vindictiveness and a simple desire for human companionship, decided to try to bring him along, he found that he was not prevented from doing so. Ginsberg himself showed no resentment at being routed out of the bed of the blond runner; possibly the succubus in Positano had spoiled for him the pleasures of human women, an outcome Jack himself had suspected in advance; but then, even without that supernatural congress, Jack's sexual life had always been that of a rather standard Don Juan, for whom every success turned sour almost instantly.

This, however, was one of those explanations which did not explain, and Baines had thought about it often before; for, as has already been observed, he liked to have his key men come equipped with handles he could grasp if the need arose. There were, the company psychologist had told him, at least three kinds of Don Juans: Freud's, whose career is a lifelong battle to hide from himself an incipient homosexuality; Lenau's, a Romantic in search of the Ideal Woman, for whom the Devil who comes for him is disgust with himself; and Da Ponte's, a man born blind to the imminence of tomorrow, and hence incapable either of love or of repentance, even on the edge of the Pit. Well, but in the end, for Baines, it did not matter which one was Jack; they all *behaved* alike.

Jack did object powerfully when he was told that the journey to Dis would have to be made entirely on foot, but this was one of the areas in which Baines discovered that the geas left him no choice.

Again, he wondered why it should be so. Did the Sabbath Goat mean to rub in the fact that the Siege of Dis had been the last gasp of secular technology? Or had it instead meant to impress upon Baines that, willy-nilly, he was about to embark upon a pilgrimage? But again, the outcome would have been the same, and that was all that mattered.

As for Jack, he still seemed to be afraid of his boss, or else still thought there was some main chance to be looked out for. Well, perhaps there was—but Baines would not have bet any shares of stock on it.

Theron Ware saw the great compound mushroom cloud go up while he was still in Flagstaff, a point to which several lucky hitchhikes and one even luckier long freight train ride had brought him. The surging growth of the cloud, the immense flares of light beyond the mountains to the west, and the repeated earth shocks left him in little doubt about what was going on; and as the cloud drifted toward him, moving inexorably from west to east as the weather usually does, he knew that it meant death for him within a very few days—as for how many thousands of others?—unless by some miracle he could find an unoccupied fallout shelter, or one whose present occupants wouldn't shoot him on sight.

And why indeed go on? The bombing showed without question that Baines's self-assumed mission to McKnight at Denver had failed, and that there was now open warfare between humanity and the demons. The notion that Theron Ware could do anything now to change that was so grandiose as to be outright pathetic. More trivially, by the time that bombing was over, no matter how it affected the demons—if at all—the whole hundred-mile-plus stretch of Death Valley National Monument would have become instantly lethal for an unprotected man to enter.

Yet Theron Ware could not yet quite believe that he was unprotected. He had come an immense distance by a traditional means which made it absolutely clear that black magic still worked; he had come almost an equal distance through a series of lucky breaks which he could not regard as the product of pure chance; and in his pocket the ruby talisman continued to emit a faint warmth which was that of no ordinary stone, natural or synthetic. Like all proverbs, Ware knew, the old saw that the Devil looks after his own was only half true; nevertheless the feeling that he had come all this way on some errand continued to persist, together with a growing conviction that he had never in fact known what it was. He would find out when he arrived; in the meantime, he was traveling on the Devil's business, and would not die until it was concluded.

He would have liked to have stopped over in Flagstaff to inspect the famous observatory where Percival Lowell had produced such complicated maps of the wholly illusory canals of Mars and where Tombaugh had discovered Pluto—and where in the sky did those planets stand, now that their gods had clashed frontally?—but under the circumstances he did not dare. He still had Grand Canyon and the Lake Mead area to cross; then, skirting northward around the Spring Mountains to the winter resort town of Death Valley, in which he hoped to be able to get some word about exactly where in the valley proper the perimeter of Nether Hell had surfaced. He had come far, but he still had far to go, and he was unlikely now to be able to hitch a ride in the direction of that roiling, flaming column of annihilation. Very well; now at last had come the time he had foreseen in the doomed farmhouse in Pennsylvania, when he would have to steal a car. He did not think that it would be difficult.

Father Domenico too had come far, and had equally good reasons to be quite certain that he would still have been in Italy had it not been for some kind of supernatural intervention. He stood now at dusk in the shadow of the 11,000-foot Telescope Peak, looking eastward and downward to where the city of Dis flamed sullenly in the shadow of the valley of death itself against the stark backdrop of the Amargosa Range. That valley had been cut by the Amargosa River, but there had been no river there within the memory of civilized man; the annual rainfall now was well under two inches.

And he was equally certain of supernatural protection. The

valley had held the world's second-ranking heat record of 134°F., but although it was immensely hotter than that down here now, Father Domenico felt only a mild glow, as though he had just stepped out of a bath. When he had first come down from the mountain, he had been horrified to find the vitrified desert washing the foothills scattered with hundreds of strange, silent, misshapen gray forms, only vaguely human at first sight, which had proven to be stricken soldiers. He had tried to minister to them, but the attempt had proven hopeless: of the bodies in the few suits he was able to investigate, most were shrunken mummies, and the rest had apparently died even more horribly. He wondered what on Earth could have happened here. His elevation from the waters to the mountain had taken place in a mystic rapture without which, indeed, it would have been impossible, but which had taken him rather out of touch with mundane events.

But whatever the answer, he had no choice but to press on. As he descended the last of the foothills, he saw on the floor of the valley, approaching him along what had once been the old watercourse and more recently a modern road, three tiny figures. Insofar as he could tell at this distance, they wore no more visible, Earthly protections against what the valley had become than he did himself. Yet they did not seem to be demons. Full of wonder, he scrambled down toward them; but when they met, and he recognized them, he wondered only that he should have been at all amazed. The meeting, he saw instantly now, had been foreordained.

"How did *you* get here?" Baines demanded at once. It was not easy to determine of whom he was asking the question, but while Father Domenico wondered whether it was worthwhile trying to explain trance levitation, and if so how he would go about it, Theron Ware said:

"I can't think of a more trivial question under the circumstances, Doctor Baines. We're here, that's the important thing—and I perceive that we are all under some kind of magical aegis, or we would all be dead. This raises the question of what we hope to accomplish, that we should be so protected. Father, may I ask what your intentions are?"

"Nothing prevents you from asking," Father Domenico said, "but you are the last human being in the world to whom I would give the answer."

"Well, I'll tell you what *my* intentions are," said Baines. "My intentions are to stay in the bottommost levels of Denver and wait for this all to blow over, if it's ever going to. One thing you learn fast in the munitions business is that it's a very good idea to stay off battlefields. But my intentions have nothing to do with the matter. I was ordered to come here by the Sabbath Goat, and here I am."

"Oh?" Ware said with interest. "He finally came for you?"

"No, I have to come to him. He broke into a closed-circuit television transmission in Denver to tell me so. He didn't even mention Jack; I only brought him along for the company, since it didn't turn out to be forbidden."

"And small thanks for that," Ginsberg said, though apparently without rancor. "If there's anything in the world that I hate, it's exercise. Vertical exercise, anyhow."

"Have either of you two seen him at all?" Baines added.

Father Domenico remained stubbornly silent, but Ware said: "Put Satanachia? No, and somehow I doubt that I will, now. I seem to have put myself under the protection of another demon, although one subordinate to the Goat. Confusion of purpose is almost the natural state among demons, but in this instance I think it couldn't have happened without direct Satanic intent."

"I was given my marching orders in the name of 'Our Father Below,'" Baines said. "If he's interested in me, the chances are that he's even more interested in you, all right. But what did you think you were up to?"

"Originally I thought I might try to intercede, or at least to plead for some sort of a cease-fire—as you were trying to do from the opposite end in Denver. But that's a dead letter now, and the result is that I have no more idea why I am here than you do. All I can say is that whatever the reason, I don't think there can be much hope in it."

"While we live, there is always hope," Father Domenico said suddenly.

The black magician pointed at the tremendous city, toward which, volitionlessly, they had been continuing to walk all this time. "To be able to see *that* at all means that we have already passed far beyond mere futility. All the sins of the Leopard, the sins of incontinence, are behind us, which means that the gate is behind us too: the gate upon which it is carven in Dirghic, LAY DOWN ALL HOPE, YOU THAT GO IN BY ME."

"We are alive," Father Domenico said stolidly, "and I utterly deny and repudiate those sins."

"You may not do so," Ware said, his voice gradually rising in intensity. "Look here, Father, this is all so mysterious, and the future looks so black, that it's ridiculous for us not to make available and to make use of any little scraps of information that we may have to share. The very symbolism of our presence here is simple, patent and ineluctable, and you as a Karcist in white magic should be the first to see it. To take the circles of Upper Hell in order, Ginsberg here is almost a type creation of the lust-dominated man; I have sold my soul for unlimited knowledge, which in the last analysis is surely nothing more than an instance of gluttony; and you have only to look around this battlefield to see that Doctor Baines is an instrument of wrath *par excellence*."

"You have skipped the Fourth Circle," Father Domenico said, "with obvious didactic intent, but your arrogance is wasted upon me. I draw no moral from it whatsoever."

"Oh, indeed? Wasn't treasure finding once the chiefest use of white magic? And isn't the monkish life—withdrawal from the snares, affairs *and duties* of the world for the sake of one's own soul—as plain a case of hoarding as one could ask for? It is in fact so egregious an example of that very sin that not even canonization remits it; I can tell you of my own certain knowledge that every single pillar saint went instantly to Hell, and of even the simple monks, none escaped except those few like Matthew Paris and Roger of Wendover who also led useful worldly lives.

"And regardless of what your fatuous friends on Monte Albano believed, there is no efficacious dispensation for the practice of white magic, because there is no such thing as white magic. It is all black, black, black as the ace of spades, and you have imperiled your immortal soul by practicing it not even for your own benefit, but on commission for others; if that does not make you a spendthrift as well as a hoarder, what would you call it?

"Think at last, Father: Why did your crucifix burst in your hands at the last minute on Black Easter? Wasn't it because you tried to use it for personal gain? What does it symbolize, if not total submission to whatever may be Willed? Yet you tried to use it—the ultimate symbol of resignation in the face of death—to save your own paltry life. Really, Father Domenico, I think the time has come for us to be frank with each other—for you as surely as for the rest of us!"

"Hear, hear," Baines said with rather a sick grin.

After six or seven paces of silence, Father Domenico said:

"I am terribly afraid you are right. I came here in the hope of forcing the demons to admit that God still lives, and I saw what I thought were indisputable signs of Divine sponsorship. Unless you are simply more subtle a casuist than any I have ever encountered before, even in print, it now appears that I had no right to think any such thing... which means that the real reason for my presence here is no less mysterious than that for yours. I cannot say that this increases my understanding any."

"It establishes a common ignorance," said Ware. "And as far as your original assumption is concerned, Father, it suggests some basic uniformity of purpose which I must admit is certainly not characteristic of demons, whatever that may mean. But I think we shall not have long to wait for the answer, gentlemen. It appears that we have arrived."

They all looked up. The colossal barbican of Dis loomed over them.

"One thing is surely clear," Father Domenico whispered. "We have been making this journey all our lives."

XII

No Beatrice sponsored them, and no Vergil led them; but as they approached the great ward, the undamaged portcullis rose, and the gates swung inward in massive silence. No demons mocked them, no Furies challenged them, no angel had to cross the Styx to bring them passage; they were admitted, simply and noncommittally.

Beyond the barbican, they found the citadel transformed. The Nether Hell of diuturnal torture, which had withstood the bombardment of Man without damage to so much as a twig in the Wood of the Suicides, was gone entirely. Perhaps in some sense it had never been there at all, but was still located where it had always been, in Eternity, not on Earth; a place still reserved for the dead. For these four still-living men, it had vanished.

In its place there stood a clean, well-lighted city like an illustration from some Utopian romance; it looked, in fact, like a cross between the city of the future in the old film *Things to Come* and a fully automated machine shop. It screamed, hammered and roared like a machine shop as well.

The grossly misshapen, semi-bestial forms of the demons had also vanished. The metropolis instead appeared to be peopled now chiefly by human beings, although their appearance could scarcely be described as normal. Male and female alike, they were strikingly beautiful; but their beauty swiftly became cloying, for except for sexual characteristics they were completely identical, as though they were all members of the same clone—one which had been genetically selected out to produce creatures modeled after the statuary fronting public buildings, or the souls in the Dante illustrations of Gustav Doré. Both sexes wore identical skirted tabards made of some gray material which looked like papier-mâché, across the breasts of which long numbers had been woven in metallically glittering script.

A second and much less numerous group wore a different uniform, vaguely military in cast, an impression reinforced by the fact that these were mostly to be seen standing stiffly at street intersections. Heroic in mold though the majority were, the minority were even more statuesque, and their common Face was evenly pleasant but stern, like that of an idealized father.

The others wore no expression at all, unless their very expressionlessness was a reflection of acute boredom—which would not have been surprising, for no one of this class seemed to have anything to do. The work of the metropolis, which seemed to be exclusively that of producing that continual, colossal din, went on behind the blank façades apparently without need of any sentient tending or intervention. They never spoke. As the four pilgrims moved onward toward the center of the city, they passed frequent exhibitions of open, public sexuality, more often than not in groups; at first Jack Ginsberg regarded these with the liveliest interest, but it soon faded as it became apparent that even this was bored and pleasureless.

There were no children; and no animals

Initially, the travelers had hesitated, when the two magicians had discovered that with the transformation they could no longer trust to Dante to show them the way, and Baines's memory of the aerial photographs had become similarly useless. They had proceeded more or less by instinct toward the center of the din. After a while, however, they found that they had been silently joined by four of the policing demons, though whether they were being led or herded never did become clear. The grimly ambiguous escort heightened the impression of a guided tour of some late nineteenth-century world-of-tomorrow which was to include awe-inspiring visits to the balloon works, the crèches, the giant telegraph center and the palace of folk arts, only to wind up in a corrective discipline hospital for the anti-social.

It was as though they were being given a preview of what the future of humanity would be like under demonic rule—not only wholly unpredictable as a foretaste, but in content as well, as if the demons were trying to put the best possible face on the matter. In so doing, they had ingenuously embodied in their citadel nothing worse than a summary and epitomization of what pre-Apocalyptic, post-industrial Man had been systematically creating for himself. St. Augustine, Goethe and Milton all had observed that the Devil, by constantly seeking evil, always did good, but here was an inversion of that happy fault: A demonstration that demons are at their worst when doing their best.

Many of Baines's most lucrative ideas for weaponry had been stolen bodily, through the intermediary of the Mamaroneck Research Institute, from the unpaid imaginations of science-fiction writers, and it was he who first gave voice to the thought:

"I always thought it'd be hell to actually have to live in a place like this," he shouted. "And now I know it."

Nobody answered him; but it was more than possible that this was because nobody had heard him.

But only the veritable Hell is forever. After some unknown but finite time, they found themselves passing between the Doric columns and under the golden architrave of that high capitol which is called Pandemonium, and the brazen doors folded open for them.

Inside, the clamor was muffled to a veiled and hollow booming, for the vast jousting field that was this hall had been made to hold the swarming audience for a panel of a thousand, but there was no one in it now besides themselves and the demon soldiers but one solitary, distant, intolerable star:

not that subsidiary triumvir Put Satanachia, the Sabbath Goat who had promised himself to them, and they to him, on Black Easter morn;

but that archetypical drop-out, the Lie that knows no End, the primeval Parent-sponsored Rebel, the Eternal Enemy, the Great Nothing itself

SATAN MEKRATRIG

There was of course no more Death Valley sunlight here, and the effect of an implacably ultramodern city with its artificial gas-glow glare was also gone. But the darkness was not quite complete. A few cressets hung blazing high in mid-air, so few that their light was spread evenly throughout the great arch of the ceiling, like the artificial sky of a planetarium dome simulating that moment between dusk and full night when only Lucifer is bright enough to be visible yet. Toward that glow they moved, and as they moved, it grew.

But the creature, they saw at last, was not the light, which shone instead upon him. The fallen cherub below it was still very nearly the same immense, brooding, cruelly deformed angelic image that Dante had seen and Milton imagined: triple-faced in yellow, red and black, bat-winged, shag-pelted, and so huge that the floor of the great hall cut him off at the breast—he must have measured five hundred yards from crown to hoof. Like the eyes, the wings were six, but they no longer beat frenziedly to stir the three winds that froze Cocytus; nor now did the six eyes weep. Instead, each of the faces—the Semitic Ignorance, the Japhetic Hatred, the Hamitic Impotence—was frozen in an expression of despair too absolute for further grief.

The pilgrims saw these things, but only with half an eye, for their attention was focused instead upon the light which both revealed and shadowed them:

The terrible crowned head of the Worm was surmounted by a halo.

XIII

The demonic guards had not followed them in, and the great Figure was motionless and uttered no orders; but in that hollowly roaring silence, the pilgrims felt compelled to speak. They looked at each other almost shyly, like school children brought to be introduced to some king or president, each wanting to be bold enough to draw attention to himself, but waiting for someone else to break the ice. Again nothing was said, but somehow agreement was arrived at: Father Domenico should speak first.

Looking aloft, but not quite into those awful countenances, the white monk said:

"Father of Lies, I thought it was my mission to come here and compel thee to speak the truth. I arrived as if by miracle, or borne by faith; and in my journeyings saw many evidences that the rule of Hell on Earth is not complete. Nor has that Goat your prince yet come for me, or for my ... colleagues here, despite his threat and promise. Then I also saw the election of your demon Pope, the very Antichrist that PUT SATANACHIA said had been dispensed with, as unnecessary to a victorious demonry. I concluded then that God was not dead after all, and someone should come into thy city to assert His continuing authority.

"I stand before thee impotent—my very crucifix was shattered in my hands on Black Easter morning—but nevertheless I charge thee and demand that thou shalt state thy limitations, and abide the course to which they hold thee."

There was no answer. After a long wait made it clear that there was not going to be, Theron Ware said next: "Master, thou knowest me well, I think; I am the last black magician in the world, and the most potent ever to practice that high art. I have seen signs and wonders much resembling those mentioned by Father Domenico, but draw from them rather different conclusions. Instead, it seems to me that the final conflict with Michael and all his host cannot be over yet—despite the obvious fact that thou hast won vast advantages already. And if this is true, then it is perhaps an error for thee to make war upon mankind, or for them to make war on thee, with the greater issue still in doubt. Since thou art still granting some of us some favors of magic, there must still exist some aid which we might give thee. Hence I came here to find out what that aid might be, and to proffer it, if it were within my powers."

No answer. Baines said sullenly:
"I came because I was ordered. But since I'm here, I may as well offer my opinion in the matter, which is much like Ware's. I tried to persuade the human generals not to attack the city, but I failed. Now that they've seen that it can't be attacked—and I'm sure they noticed that you didn't wipe out all their forces when you had the chance—I might have better luck. At least I'll try again, if it's of any use to you.
"I can't imagine any way we could help you carry the war to Heaven, since we were no good against your own local fortress. And besides, I prefer to remain neutral. But getting our generals off your back might relieve you of a nuisance, if you've got more serious business still afoot. If that's not good enough, don't blame me. I didn't come here of my own free will."

The terrible silence persisted, until at last even Jack Ginsberg was forced to speak.
"If you're waiting for me, I have no suggestions," he said. "I guess I'm grateful for past favors, too, but I don't understand what's going on and I didn't want to get involved. I was only doing my job, but as far as my private life goes, I'd just as soon be left to work it out for myself from now on. As far as I'm concerned, it's nobody's business but my own."

Now, at last, the great wings stirred slightly; and then, the three faces spoke. There was no audible voice, but as the vast lips moved, the words formed in their minds, like sparks crawling along logs in a dying fire.

"O yee of little faith," the Worm set on,
"Yee whose coming fame had bodied forth
A hope archchemic even to this Deep
That Wee should be amerced of golden Throne,
The which to Us a rack is, by thine alchymie,
Is this thy sovran Reason? this the draff,
Are these sollicitations all the sum
And sorrie Substance of thine high renoune?
Art thou accomplisht to so mean an end
After such journeyings of flame and dole
As once strook doun Heav'n's angels? Say it so,
In prosie speach or numerous prosodie,
Wee will not be deceav'd; so much the rather
Shall Wee see yee rased from off the bord
'Twixt Hell and Heav'n, as the fearful mariner,
Ingled by the wave 'mongst spume and rock,
Sees craft and hope alike go all to ruin,
Yet yields up not his soul, than Wee shall yield
The last, supreme endeavour of this fearfull Jarr.

"Yet how to body forth to thy blind eyes,
Who have not poets' blindnesse, or the night
Shed by black suns, 'thout which to tell the tale
Of earth its occupation by the demon breed
Is sole remaining hearth, but to begin?
O 'suaging Night, console Mee now! and hold
My Demy-godhood but a little while
Abeyanc'd from its death in Godhood's dawn!

"O yee of little faith, Wee tell thee this:
Indeed our God is dead; or dead to us.
But in some depth of measure beyond grasp

Remains His principle, as doth the sight
Of drowsy horoscoper, much bemus'd
By vastnesses celestial and horrid
To his tinie system, when first he looks
Through the optic glass at double stars,
Some residuum apprehend; so do we now.
O happie matrix! for there is naught else
That all are left with. It in this inheres,
That Good is independent, but the bad
Cannot alone survive; the evil Deed
Doth need the Holie Light to lend it Sense
And apprehension; for the Good is free
To act or not, while evill hath been will'd
Insensate and compulsive to bring Good
Still greater highths unto, as climber see'th,
From toil and suff'ring to th'uttermost Alp,
Best th'unattainable islands of the skye.

"In this yee Sinners are in harmonie,
Antient and grand, though meanlie did yee move
About your severall ends. Since first this subject,
Thou, thaumaturgist Blacke, and thou,
O merchant peccant to the deaths of fellowe men,
Contrived in evill all thy predecessors human,
But save Judas I was wont to gnaw before,
T'outdo, by willingnesse to plunge
All mankinde in a night's Abysse
Only for perverse aestheticke Joye
And Thrill of Masterie, there then ensu'd
That universall Warr in which the victorie
Hath faln to Hellish host, so Wee rejoyc'd;
Yet hold! for once releas'd from Paynes
Decreed to be forever, all our Band
Of demons foul, who once were angels bright
Conceiv'd in simpler time and ever since
Entomb'd amidst the horrors of the Pit,

Did find the world of men so much more foul
E'en than in the fabulous reign of witches
That all bewilder'd fell they and amazed.
Yet after hastie consult, they set to,
To preach and practise evill with all pow'r,
Adhering to grounded rules long understood,
A Greshamite oeconomium.

                                But eftsoons
That vacuous space where once Eternall Good
Had dwelt demanded to be filled. Though God
Be dead, His Throne remains. And so below
As 'twas above, last shall be first, and Wee,
Who by the Essenes' rule are qualified
Beyond all remaining others, must become—
In all protesting agonie—the chief
Of powers for Good in all the Universe
Uncircumscribed; but let yee not forget,
Already Good compared to such as thee,
Whose evill remains will'd! And as for Us,
What doth it matter what Wee most desire?
While chainèd in the Pit, Wee were condemn'd
To be eternall, but paroll'd to Earth
Were once more caught by Change; and how
Could Wickednesse Incorporeal grow still worse?
And so, behold! Wee are a God.

                                      But not
Perhaps The God. Wee do not know the end.
Perhaps indeed Jehovah is not dead,
But mere retir'd, withdrawn or otherwise
Contracted hath, as *Zohar* subtle saith,
His Essence Infinite; and, Epicurean, waits
The outcome vast with vast indifference.
Yet natheless His universe requires
That all things changing must tend t'ward His state.
    If, then, wee must proclaim His Rôle historic

Abandon'd in Deific suicide,
Why this *felo de Se* except to force
That part on Man—who fail'd it out of hand?
Now, as Wee sought to be in the Beginning,
SATAN is God; and in Mine agonie
More just a God and wrathfuller by far
Than He Who thunder'd down on Israel!

    "Yet not for ever, though our rule will seem
For ever. Man, O Man, I beg of you,
Take, O take from mee this Cup away!
I cannot bear it. You, and onely you,
You alone, alone can God become,
As always He intended. This downfall
Our mutual Armageddon here below
Is punishment dire enough, but for your Kinde
A worse awaits; for you must rear yourselves
As ready for the Resurrection. I
Have slammed that door behind; yours is to come.
On that far future Day, I shall be there,
The burning Keys to put into your hands.

    "I, SATAN MEKRATRIG, can no longer bear
This deepest, last and bitterest of all
My fell damnations: That at last I know
I never wanted to be God at all;
And so, by winning all, All have I lost."

(*The great hall of Pandemonium dissolves, and with it the Citadel of Dis, leaving the four men standing in a modern road in the midst of the small town of Badwater. It is early morning in the desert, and still cold. All traces of the recent battle also have vanished.*

(*The four look at each other, with gradually growing wonder, as though each were seeing the others for the first time. Each one finally starts a sentence, but is unable to complete it*):

FATHER DOMENICO: I think ...

BAINES: I believe...
WARE: I hope...
(*They look about, noting the disappearance of the battlefield. After all else that has happened, they do not question this; it does not even surprise them.*)
GINSBERG: I...love.

CURTAIN

Author's Afterword

This novel, though it is intended to be able to stand as an independent entity, is a sequel to another with nearly the same cast of characters, called *Black Easter* or *Faust Aleph-Null* (Doubleday, New York, 1968).

These two books, considered as a unit, in turn make up the second volume of a trilogy under the overall title of AFTER SUCH KNOWLEDGE. The first volume is a historical novel called *Doctor Mirabilis* (Faber and Faber, London, 1964); the last, a science-fiction novel called *A Case of Conscience* (Faber and Faber, London, 1959). These two volumes are independent of each other and of *Black Easter* and *The Day After Judgment*, except for subject matter; that is, they are intended to dramatize different aspects of an ancient philosophical question which is voiced by Baines in Chapter VIII of the present work.

As before, the books of magic cited in the text all actually exist (although mostly in manuscript), and the magical rituals and diagrams are all taken from them (although in no case are they complete). The characters and events, on the other hand, are entirely my own invention, as are all the details about the Strategic Air Command.

JAMES BLISH

Harpsden (Henley)
Oxon., England
1970

Milton Keynes UK
Ingram Content Group UK Ltd.
UKHW030738071024
449371UK00005B/361